Teen Targets

Teen Targets

CHARLOTTESVILLE TEENS TARGETED

JIM SARGENT AND AUDREY DEICHMANN

Published by Jim Sargent
https://www.jimsargentbooks.com/

Cover by Inez Farrell
Layout design by Christianna Deichmann

Paperback ISBN: 979-8-993109-0-22

ePub ISBN: 979-8-993109-0-39
Library of Congress Control Number:

Dedication

For the ones who came before us, the ones who walk beside us, and the ones who will carry the torch next.

This book was dreamed up across three generations: from father to daughter to granddaughter.

May it inspire young hearts to believe in their stories—and in each other.

With love,

From our family to yours.
Teen Targets

Jim Sargent and Audrey Deichmann

Chapter 1

World War, Changes at Home, and Teens

Looking up at the dazzling sun just before noon on the second Saturday in April, I had no idea a dangerous adventure was in store for my family. Walking from the field to our two-story farmhouse house after nearly two hours of hoeing our acre of vegetables, I felt worn out.

During these wartime days most farms have a chunk of land devoted to what President Franklin Roosevelt calls "Victory Gardens." In fact, we're growing more vegetables this year than we did in 1942, due to higher demand, but our apple orchards will produce about the same.

At high school, the teachers are making a big deal out of how World War II is changing our lives. We have to live with rationing foods like sugar, coffee, meat and necessities like soap, gasoline, and paper. Another big change came in February of 1942 when the government ordered the auto industry to convert to war production. That means we won't have new cars to buy until after the war. Of course, sports are affected. I saw a story in the newspaper last week predicting that big league baseball would end for the duration due to the military's manpower demands.

Just as I took my long hop onto our low back porch, Natalia opened the screen door from the kitchen.

Stepping outside, she looked at me with anxious eyes. I lifted my eyebrows, and she smiled. My sister likes to flash her coy smile.

"James, have you got time to look at the essay I'm writing for Miss DeRoche in English 10?"

I started to reply, but she cut me off. "I know what you're thinking, Big Brother. I should be making myself useful around here on Saturday, right?" She shook her head once, making me wonder what was going on. "But you get really good grades in English, or I wouldn't ask."

Her expression told me to just go along, so I did. "Sure, why not? First, I have to wash up. Working in the garden makes me sweat. You go ahead, and I'll be with you in a couple of minutes."

Satisfied, Nat turned and made a bee-line through the kitchen to the stairway at the end of the dining room. She didn't even speak to Aunt Cora, who was sitting at the long linen-covered table and making a grocery list. At the sink, I grabbed a damp cloth and wiped my forehead and washed my hands. I grinned, because it always feels good to be clean.

When I turned to face her, Aunt Cora gave me her sweet smile, her special way of lifting your spirits. "James, dear. Do you think you could drive me to Jack's Grocery after lunch? I need to buy a few items."

Again she smiled. "I really need more ingredients for baking pies."

I smiled too, because you have to like Aunt Cora. She's always concerned about us. She cooks almost every meal. She keeps the house as clean as a whistle. She listens when you want someone to hear your problems. Actually, she's *more* than an aunt. She even looks a lot like Mom used to look. Aunt Cora has the same brown eyes, the same brown hair, with a bit of gray added, the same thin lips, and her personality is so pleasant. She has a way of making you feel better when she talks to you. I remember our mother having that way about her too, so maybe we should expect that from her older sister.

"Sure, I'll drive you, Aunt Cora. Right now I need to run up to Nat's room and look over a paper she's writing for English." I grinned. "Anyhow, I like driving."

Again Aunt Cora smiled, and her brown eyes twinkled. "You are *so* helpful, James, especially since now you're driving your father's old pickup."

Nodding, she rose from the table and headed to the cupboard, and I went into the dining room and climbed the staircase. In the upstairs hallway, I turned toward Nat's bedroom, the last one on the right. All of the five bedrooms have a cupola with a window, so they're all bright and airy. Of course, Dad's room, the master bedroom facing the fields to the west, is the largest. His dark wooden dresser and chair are made of walnut, like the furniture in the other bedrooms. We have what used to be another large bedroom downstairs, but years ago it was converted to a den.

When I entered Nat's room, she gave me the silent sign, a forefinger to the lips and handed me a folded page. "Read this letter I just received from Karl Ellis, who lives in New York City."

When I looked her in the eye, she sighed. "Just *read it*, James, especially the ending."

I scanned Karl's letter. His writing was cramped, but his message was interesting: *I had a visit one week ago from an older student, Ernie Herbert, who traveled over here from England. Ernie hates the war. He wants to get away from the bombing, the suffering, the shortages, and the rest of it. He's considering enrolling here at NYU, and he says a counselor advised him to talk to a few students. I guess that's why he showed up at my apartment.*

We talked about college stuff like classes and majors and places to live. I told him I lived for a while last summer with an uncle in Charlottesville, but I never gave his name. I just said it was because I was thinking about going to the University of Virginia. He asked if I liked it there, and I did. I told him the uncle passed away, but I didn't mention that Uncle Otto was a secret Nazi. I just told Ernie it was less expensive for me to live here with my father and attend NYU.

I guess my story prompted Ernie to tell me his. It turns out he grew up in Portsmouth, England, with his mother, Ann Arnold, who came from London. He never knew his father, and his mother said the husband abandoned her years ago. They moved to Munich, Germany, and lived there a few years when Ernie was younger because the schools are supposed to be very good. When the Germans invaded Poland in 1939, Ernie and his Mom left Germany, crossed the English Channel, and moved to Plymouth on the southwest coast. She has a brother living there, and he took them in. But after a couple of years, Ernie landed a job as a seaman on a Lend-Lease ship bound for New York. On the ship he bunked next to a seaman from Roanoke, who said he loved the University of Virginia because his older brother went there and later became a teacher.

When Ernie left, he was talking about moving to Charlottesville. Natalia, you and James live there, so I thought you might like to know about this bright young Englishman. By the way, if I can earn a little extra money, I'm going to visit you this summer. In case you need to call, my phone number is on the back. Sincerely, Karl

I noticed the phone number, folded the letter, and handed it back to Nat. We looked at each other knowingly. "Is Karl telling us about this guy Ernie, or about himself, Karl, visiting us this summer?"

"Well, I'm not sure, James. But I'm wondering about this English guy who looked him up."

I nodded. "Well, maybe we'll hear more from Karl. But for now, I'm hungry! Aunt Cora's making lunch, and afterward, she wants me to take her grocery shopping."

"Okay, I'll be right down," Nat said. As I turned to leave, she opened the right drawer of her desk and placed the letter inside, next to the blue leather bound *My Diary* that she started keeping a year ago after her first encounter with Otto Herman. I descended the stairs thinking, *Karl still likes Nat, but he must have doubts about Ernie Herbert, or he wouldn't have written the letter.*

II

Following lunch, Aunt Cora came out with me and we got into our old black Chevrolet pickup parked by the house. Earlier I had moved the truck from behind our large red barn, where we usually park it, to the driveway. After Aunt Cora climbed in and closed the passenger door, we motored out to the road. I looked both ways before turning toward town. We hadn't driven far when out of the corner of my eye I noticed Cora looked nervous.

The pick-up rides kind of rough, but we use it mainly for running errands. Also, Dad is letting me drive to school and to baseball this spring. So far I haven't taken our blue 1939 Chevrolet on a date, but I think that's coming soon. As for our aunt, the truck provides her a way to go into town and shop, when Dad has gone somewhere in the car. Since I'm finally old enough to drive and I don't have much experience, I guess riding with me is what makes her nervous.

Hoping to lighten her mood, I asked, "Are you having a good day, Aunt Cora?"

She nodded, but she didn't take her eyes off the road. After a few moments, I said casually, "You want to go to Jack's, right?"

She nodded, but didn't smile. We were traveling 35 miles per hour, which is the government's "Victory Speed Limit." In fact, by 1943 America was in full swing with conserving resources, including rationing gasoline, which led to lower speed limits. Still, I eased off the gas pedal, slowing to 30 mph.

Reflecting on rationing, I figure what affects Americans the most is food. Even if you can grow much of what your family needs, you still need to figure out the complicated rationing system imposed in early 1943 by the federal Office of Price Administration, or the OPA.

I understand it works like this: The OPA determined that every person receives 48 blue points for processed food per month, and counting Aunt Cora, a family of four like ours receives 192 points. The points come to families as books of stamps. Every city, town, and village has local rationing boards operated by citizens who volunteer to hand out the books of stamps.

Tires were rationed first, not long after Pearl Harbor was bombed. Early in 1942, consumers like us were no longer allowed to buy new tires for their car or truck. You had to patch a blown inner tube or have an old tire retreaded. Of course, the doctors, nurses, policemen, firemen, owners of buses and delivery vans, all of them essential for the economy to function, could buy new tires. But they still have to apply to their local rationing board.

The rationing program seems like a nightmare. But to win the war, I guess America must produce more food. And we need more jeeps, trucks, tanks, airplanes, guns, and ammunition to equip our Army, Navy, and Air Force. As far as I can tell, there's no end in sight for rationing.

We cruised into the south side of town, and I turned right on Main Street toward Jack's Grocery. Even though it's Saturday, I found a parking place almost in front. After we parked, Aunt Cora looked at me and offered her trademark smile. We climbed out and went into Jack's.

Inside, I ran into Herb Jenkowski. Wearing a white sailor's cap, he has a white apron over his white shirt, blue bow tie, and pale blue slacks. He works there on Saturdays bagging groceries, stocking shelves, and whatever else the proprietor wants done.

Herb was standing near the second checkout counter telling a stocky fiftyish woman with curly brown hair where to find the baking soda. Looking at him, she turned and told a slender gray-haired man to go get a box. Rolling his eyes, he headed for aisle three as Aunt Cora picked up a shopping basket. The graying man returned with the prize, the couple lined up at the second counter, and she plopped down her red purse to dig into it for the money and the April stamp book. The cashier, a black-haired girl whom I recognized from Jefferson High, just waited.

Herb grinned when he saw me, and I joined him near the ice cream counter. I know he's hoping to work 20 hours a week this summer so he can save up to go to college after we graduate from Jefferson next spring. Standing there, we talked about our first home game with Robert E. Lee High, from Staunton, next Friday.

At that point two boys about five or six years old came up to Herb and asked for ice cream. I watched him move behind the counter holding tubs of vanilla, chocolate, and strawberry ice cream, grab a scoop out of a glass of water, and scoop a large dip for each cone. You should have seen the boys' eyes! Playing along, Herb winked. "You kids come back the next time you want plenty of ice cream, right?!"

That's Herb for you. He likes kids, and people, and sports, especially baseball, and he's a great catcher. Of course, he likes girls, has a good work ethic, and respects adults. He's a real friend, and it's hard not to like him. A ruggedly handsome guy with a muscular physique, he's got black eyes, black hair, and a low voice. He and I are the same height, six feet tall, but he's heavier than me, maybe 180.

After getting their ice cream, the two happy boys hurried away, and Herb and I got together and talked about the upcoming game. Lee is rated one class below Jefferson, but they always give us a run for the money. Last year we beat them, 5-2, thanks to Jefferson putting together several base hits and walks in the sixth and seventh innings.

Herb grinned. "You gonna take Linda Lawton to the movies tonight? She sure has turned into one good lookin' brunette with her long brown hair!" He winked. "I'm not the only guy sayin' that, either!"

I nodded. "Yeah, her family lives in town, and I called her Thursday night. Her father wanted to know if I was old enough to drive our car to pick her up. Of course, I'm 16 and I've got my driver's license. But Dad wasn't home, so I couldn't ask him about taking the Chevy."

Herb raised his eyebrows. "Geez, James. You *can* get your dad's cool blue sedan, right? I mean, what's with ol' man Lawton? Won't he let his daughter go if you come in the *truck*?"

"I don't know, but Linda was supposed to call me last night. Are you going tonight?"

Looking around, he studied me. "Okay, James. I'm tellin' you, but it goes no further, right?"

I nodded, and he continued: "The other day I talked to Iris Hofner, that auburn honey in the tenth grade, and she said yes." His black eyes looked bright. "Get this, pal. We're gonna see *Casablanca* with Humphrey Bogart at the Lafayette. I'm taking Iris to the 5:00 show. We'll get hamburgers afterward, and, well, who knows?" He winked. "By the way, I figure a dollar and a half ought to cover the cost."

"Way to go, Herb! Listen, if I hear from Linda, I'll tell her I want to see *Casablanca* too …"

"Hey, *Jenkowski*!"

I heard the loud voice, turned, and saw a lean middle-aged man about five-foot-eleven with sandy hair outfitted with a long white shopkeeper's apron over his clothes. Considering his white shirt and red polka dot bow tie, I guessed he was Mister Johnson, the proprietor.

He looks like someone used to exercising authority, and he was staring at Herb like he'd committed a crime. "Did you clean up that mess in front of the meat counter?"

"No, sir, Mister Johnson, but I was just on my way to grab a broom and get it done."

Looking over at the two checkout counters, I saw Aunt Cora in the first aisle next to the cash register paying the clerk. I hurried over just as Wanda Winston called from near the manager's office. "James, when you get back home, please tell Nat I really need to talk to her!"

You can't miss Wanda with her fiery red hair, freckles, and ivory skin. I smiled and nodded at Wanda, and then I met Aunt Cora up front. She pointed to two large brown bags jammed with groceries. Grabbing the bags off the counter, we headed for the truck. As I started the engine, I looked at her. "Did you find everything you needed?"

"Well, your father likes Campbell's Tomato Soup, and I found two cans, but they ran out of Chicken Noodle. Zeke does *not* like Pepper Pot, and they never seem to have enough Chicken Noodle!"

I smiled, and Cora looked at me for a few seconds. "I do hope he likes my choices, because I want him to be *pleased* that I'm making a difference for all of you."

We drove home, and Aunt Cora seemed to relax on the way. I braked beside the house, switched off the engine, and slipped out of the pickup. Grabbing the two bags, I followed her inside. Dad was standing at the sink washing up. After drying off with a hand towel, he smiled at Aunt Cora, and she smiled sweetly in return. Watching them, I hoped Linda would call soon.

III

Later that afternoon, I was sitting at the kitchen table chatting with Aunt Cora and Dad when the wall telephone next to the back door rang. As I stood up, I noticed the kitchen clock showed the time was 2:35. I moved over and lifted the black receiver. After telling the caller it was the Baker residence, I heard Linda's pleasant voice. "You thought I forgot about you, but I didn't. I forgot to check with Mom, but she knows you, and she's happy about my date."

Actually, I had wondered about her mother, but I skipped that. "Really, I didn't think you forgot. Anyway, I checked the movies at the Lafayette, and *Casablanca* is playing. A while ago I saw my buddy

Herb Jenkowski at the grocery store, and he and his date are going to the 5:00 show."

"Oh, James! That would be so neat! I'd love to go!"

She made me smile. "That's great! Suppose I pick you up around 4:30. We can meet them at the theater, get our tickets, and find the seats."

She agreed, and after a couple of comments, we hung up. Afterward, I began whistling "Boogie Woogie Bugle Boy." When I turned around, Aunt Cora and Dad were smiling.

"Well, well, James," she said. "So, you and Linda Lawton are going to the movies tonight."

"Yes, we're going." Smiling, I turned to Dad. "I may not have mentioned this, but it would be great if I could take the Chevy."

He grinned widely. "Sure, James. Go ahead. Just make sure you don't use any more gas than you have to. You know the red tape we go through with rationing these days."

"No problem, Dad, and I should be home around 10:00. We're probably going to stop for a milkshake or a Coca-Cola with Herb and his date. After that, I might stay a few minutes at Linda's house and talk to her parents."

Grabbing the ring with the Chevrolet keys from the hook next to the back door, I walked outside. The four-door sedan was still parked where Dad left it. I wanted to see if a wash job was needed, but the car looks swell. The bright sunlight made the blue paint look shiny. Opening the driver's door, I slipped in and sat behind the steering wheel. From the first time I saw this '39 Master Deluxe, I thought the dashboard looked more modern compared to the dash in the 1937 Chevrolet we used to own. I smiled, realizing this car ran twice as smooth as the pickup.

I rubbed my hand over the blue seat covers. Thinking ahead to after the movies, I'd like to take Linda on a ride somewhere. *I can still make it home by 10:00*, I thought.

Walking back to the house, I needed to take a bath since I hadn't taken one this morning. Dad and Aunt Cora had gone into the living room, probably relaxing in their favorite easy chairs. I could hear them talking about church tomorrow. Aunt Cora sounded happy about a blue dress she just received in the mail from Sears, Roebuck, thanks to the good ol' mail order catalog. I'll bet thousands of farm families depend on that catalog.

The next couple of hours flew past, with me taking a bath, watching Aunt Cora press my khaki slacks and navy blue shirt, and hearing about Nat writing someone a letter. After dressing carefully and shining my black school shoes, I enjoyed a sandwich and a cup of coffee that Aunt Cora fixed. Feeling spiffy, I strolled out to the Chevy, got in, and started the engine.

I drove thirty minutes into Charlottesville and to the Lawton's two-story white house, just off Main Street. When I parked at the curb, the dashboard clock said 4:35. Walking up to the porch, I knocked on the door. After a few moments, Linda appeared. *She looks great* flashed across my mind.

Smiling, she opened the screen door and invited me inside. She wore a light green dress with white lace trim, a white collar, and a white belt. She had her long brown hair brushed and curled at the bottom. Seeing her captivating face, bright eyes, and easy smile, I couldn't help but stare. In a moment I heard myself saying, "Geez, Linda. You look *swell*."

She beamed, and at that moment her mother appeared. She looks like an older version of her daughter. She's about the same 5'3" with the brown hair, only cut shorter, the brown eyes, only wiser, and pleasant demeanor, but older by maybe twenty years.

"Now you two need to be home by 9:30, you know," Missus Lawton observed, looking us up and down. "Don't forget. Tomorrow we need to be at church at 9:45."

Assuring her that we would be home on time, Linda added, "Mom, we're going to see *Casablanca*, with

Humphrey Bogart and Ingrid Bergman. Afterward, we'll probably have a soda or a shake with James' friend Herb and his date."

The two of us walked out to the car, and I held the door for her. It took ten minutes to reach the Lafayette and park in the side lot. Holding hands, we walked around in front. I saw a long line at the ticket window, and Herb and Iris were standing near the back. When we approached, the girls seemed to evaluate each other, but all the while they smiled sweetly.

Herb and I made the introductions. I see Iris at school almost daily, and Herb, grinning, called her "good-looking." Her reddish-brown hair is stylish, her brown eyes wide, her personality outgoing, and like Linda, she looks really nice in her clothes. I felt proud to be there.

Once we bought the tickets, we walked through the lobby past several people buying popcorn and drinks at the counter. I noticed a tall sandy-haired, blue-eyed young man with a bag of popcorn looking at the posters for Coming Attractions. I saw him taking more than one look at us as we walked past.

His appearance rang a bell, but before I could think about why, the stocky attendant in the maroon uniform at the left door asked for the tickets. Herb passed me his tickets, I handed the guy all four. Nodding, he tore off the stubs, handed them back, and we went inside.

The floor sloped gradually down toward the large silver screen. In the semi-darkness, the theater looked more than half full.

We spotted good seats a few rows from the back, and Herb, holding Iris' hand, led the way As we settled into our seats, with the girls beside each other and the guys flanking them, Linda whispered we should go to the Timberlake Drug Store on Main Street afterward. Herb and Iris, nodding, both agreed.

In no time the lights went down, and the *MovieTone News* filled our eyes and ears. Many of the scenes came from conflicts in the world war. I disliked people running in fear from the German Army in Tunisia and from Japanese troops in the Solomon Islands. A hush came over the audience when the movie opened with a spinning globe, a patriotic French song, and a voice-over intoning the importance of Casablanca, a port city in Morocco ruled by the French.

Once the action began, Linda and Iris started whispering about what they were seeing. Later, Herb and I each offered some quiet comments. The movie is what they call a "romantic drama," and Humphrey is the big star. The plot is set during World War II, and "Bogie," as he's often called, portrays Rick Blaine, an expatriate American who runs the Cafe American in Casablanca.

Out of the corner of my eye I saw Herb slip his arm around Iris right after Ingrid Bergman entered the cafe. Taking the cue, I slid my arm around Linda. She smiled at me, so I knew she liked it. The girls enjoyed the "lovebird" part of the story, but the suspense and mystery just kept growing.

The movie really held our attention with the story and the characters and the twists and turns. Near the end, when Rick steals the show, I touched Linda's arm. She looked at me with those big brown eyes, and I thought, *She wants me to kiss her*. Herb had the same idea, but Iris held his hand in hers and kept her eyes on the screen. I didn't want to seem too forward, so I just smiled at Linda. But I knew she was feeling the same as me, and the right time would come.

In a few minutes *The End* flashed across the screen, the credits were rolling, the romantic mood faded, and the lights came up. I rubbed my eyes as all four of us stood up, made our way to the aisle, and joined dozens of others walking up each aisle and leaving through the swinging doors. In the lobby it looked like most of Charlottesville couldn't wait to see the next show!

We got into the car, and following Herb in his father's black 1940 Ford sedan, we drove to Timberlake Drugs. By then the time was 7:40 and darkness was filtering down around us like black grains of sand. Inside Timberlake's, we found seats at the rear lunch counter with its cherry red bar. We all ordered milkshakes, cherry for Herb and Iris, chocolate for Linda, and strawberry for me.

We chatted about the movie while enjoying the shakes, and it seemed like each of us saw a slightly different film. I started it by observing, "Rick's character is so cynical, and you wonder why. Later, it turns out that Ilsa, or Ingrid Bergman, once left Rick in Paris without any explanation, and makes you sympathize more with Rick."

Iris frowned. She told us her family came to America from northern Italy in the 1920s. "The Fascists looked decent in the early 1920s, but fascism turned out to be bad for the whole country. You couldn't blame people for wanting to leave for America. Later on, my grandfather moved our family here to avoid serving in the Italian Army. I've heard stories, but," and her eyes twinkled, "maybe another time!"

Linda smiled. "That's interesting, Iris, and I'm sure the Fascists were tough on other people. I was touched at the end when Rick gave up his chance of being happy with Ilsa and insisted that she leave with her husband on the plane."

As that kind of talk went back and forth, I knew the evening was a big success. When Herb winked at me as we stood up to leave, I knew he felt the same way.

Linda and I climbed into the Chevrolet, and I started the engine. The dashboard clock showed 8:45. My mind raced ahead, and we drove toward her house without a word. Parking across the street from the Lawton's, I looked at her and smiled. "This has been a really good time. That movie just grabs your attention, and I felt like the love triangle sealed it."

Taking my hand, she gave me a dreamy gaze. Dad used to say, *Don't try to kiss your girl on the first date.* Eyeing her, I said quietly, "Maybe we ought to get you inside in plenty of time."

Moments later we hugged on the front porch, even though the porch light seemed bright as a lighthouse. "I'll see you at school next week, and maybe next Saturday …"

"Yes, James, next weekend." Reaching up, she kissed me on the cheek. "I want to see another movie … *with you.*"

With her brown eyes focused on my eyes, she flashed a smile, turned, and went inside. I walked down the two steps and out to the car. Starting the engine, I sat and looked at their house for a long minute. Finally, I drove away. On the way home I kept grinning and thinking about Linda and her dreamy eyes and her sweet lips.

Chapter 2

Springtime and Helen LaSalle

A few minutes after noon on Sunday, we emerged from the peaked double door entrance to Calvary Presbyterian Church into the bright sunlight. Aunt Cora smiled and said hello to the Reverend Charles Benjamin, who likes greeting everyone. Right behind her, Dad smiled, shook hands vigorously with him and they exchanged a few words. Outside, people filled the church plaza, chatting, laughing, and making plans. A few minutes later, Dad, Cora, Natalia, and I headed for our Chevrolet parked across the street.

As we climbed into the car with Dad and Cora in the front, I looked over and saw Reverend Benjamin talking with an attractive dark-haired woman who looked familiar. Nat leaned close and whispered, "Helen LaSalle is her name. I heard she's been the church secretary for six months."

I nodded. Both of us had noticed her attending Sunday services before, but I didn't know her name. Usually she sits in the back pew on the right. She has a little girl of maybe five years old, and she clings to her mother like she's a lifeline to tomorrow. Today the girl looks cute in a pink dress.

As Dad started the car, Aunt Cora asked where we should eat. With the engine idling, he indicated

Sammy's Diner near the University of Virginia would be good. Aunt Cora said, "Don't you think too many students will be running in and out of there?"

While the lunch discussion proceeded, Missus LaSalle and her daughter crossed the street in front of our car, and they headed along the sidewalk. I noticed that the mother looked quite attractive in her tight navy blue dress with a white collar. I saw Dad looking her over too.

Helen is a medium-sized woman with sleek black hair brushed into a bob, and she look maybe five-two or five-three. Her elegant face is graced with blue eyes, a straight nose, and full lips, and she's using maroon lipstick. Looking a lot like a fashion model, she has a graceful walk. I saw Nat looking her over too.

"The food at Sammy's is top notch," our father finally said, and Aunt Cora agreed. Dad shifted the Chevy, and in less than ten minutes we were parked at the curb close to Sammy's.

The popular diner is located near "The Corner" on the edge of the university's campus. The four of us climbed out and went inside, and we found the place jumping! We did manage to find a booth on one side, but only because the family using it stood up to leave.

The minute we sat down, a dark-faced six-foot waiter in his 40s hurried over, wiped off the table with a white cloth, and handed us foldout menus. "Welcome, folks. I'm Abraham. How are y'all doing today?"

"Hello, Abraham," Dad smiled at him. "We're out for a good meal, and I'll bet you can help us with that."

"I'll be pleased to serve you today." Abraham smiled broadly, and his black eyes sparkled. "We're getting busy, but I'm ready!"

Bowing his head, he revealed a bald spot surrounded by black kinky hair. Looking at us, he was ready t take our orders. Dad asked for a slice of roast beef, mashed potatoes, and green peas, and Nat and I ordered the same. Aunt Cora, studying the menu, sniffed daintily. She ordered a pork chop, asparagus, potato salad, and iced tea. Smiling, Dad asked for ice tea all around.

Although the tables and booths all around were virtually filled, Abraham soon returned with the food. As we were eating, I noticed Helen LaSalle entering the door and holding her little girl by the hand. A stubby crewcut waiter led them to a table on the opposite side of the room. Once seated, Missus LaSalle glanced our way. In a few moments, Dad, taking a forkful of mashed potatoes, saw them. "Oh, look. There's Missus LaSalle, and her daughter, from church."

He waved and smiled at them. Nat saw his expression better than I did, but out of the corner of my eye, I saw Missus LaSalle return the smile. As if on cue, the daughter got up from the table and pointed our way. Several couples near our booth looked to see why the kid was pointing, and Dad's face began to redden. All the while Aunt Cora ate serenely, seeming to pay no attention to the mother and daughter.

But Aunt Cora's mood quickly changed. She turned to Dad and declared, "I don't feel like dessert today." She placed her tableware on the empty plate. "Zeke, do you mind if we leave? I would like to take care of a few things this afternoon before dinner. Tonight I want to listen to *Fibber McGee and Molly* on the radio. It's my favorite radio program."

At that point the little girl appeared beside Dad, peering innocently up at him. In a small voice, she said, "Are you Mister Baker?" Before he could reply, she added, "My name is Joyce. My Mother thinks you are handsome."

The girl's comment surprised us, notably Aunt Cora, who gasped, and Nat, who stared open-mouthed at the kid. A few moments later, Missus LaSalle arrived at our table with her cheeks flushed. She grabbed her daughter's hand like she had escaped confinement.

Missus LaSalle backed up a step. "Oh, my! I do hope Joyce has not embarrassed me again with one of the wild comments she just *loves* making!"

An awkward silence followed, but Aunt Cora broke it by standing up with a no-nonsense look on her face.

Looking at her, Dad stood up, and Nat and me all but sprang to our feet.

"Why, I'm sorry, Missus LaSalle," Aunt Cora said primly. "Your daughter did come over and make *some* remarks, but there's no *problem*." As Dad grinned awkwardly, our aunt added, "We're just heading for home to take a little afternoon break."

"Oh, I do hope Joyce hasn't stepped out of line." Brushing a lock of black hair away from one eye, Missus LaSalle looked us over. I thought Aunt Cora was going to make a curt comment, but she surprised me.

"Why, little Joyce … is that her name? She just made the kind of silly remark little girls, *and* little boys, can pull out of the hat and embarrass us. But *please*, pay no attention to that."

I could see Aunt Cora was anxious to leave, but Dad wasn't ready. "We're heading back to our farm," he stated, with an exaggerated smile. "Maybe we'll see you next week at church."

Picking up her purse, Aunt Cora grabbed Nat's hand, and the two of them headed for the door. "Come along, Natalia" I heard our aunt say. "Let us enjoy our little walk."

I glanced at Dad, and he shrugged. After a few moments, he took off after Cora and Nat, and I followed suit. Later, when all of us were climbing into the car, Nat winked at me and slipped into the back seat from the driver's side, and I got after her. Relaxing, I glanced at Aunt Cora in the passenger's seat. She appeared to be watching two little girls dance along the sidewalk.

Never a dull moment, at least not in our family, I thought. As our car headed out of town, I knew Nat couldn't wait to spill her information. I smiled to myself because we both had plenty of food for thought. When we arrived home, Dad and Aunt Cora climbed out and walked into the back door, but I didn't hear either of them speak.

II

In the kitchen, Nat and I looked at each other, Dad strolled into the dining room and went upstairs, and Aunt Cora, watching him, placed her purse on the table. Moving over to the sink, she filled a glass with water and made a show of drinking it. Looking at us, she said airily, "Zeke has gone up to change. I suppose he'll be busy all afternoon."

Finishing the water, Aunt Cora placed the glass in the sink. Turning our way, she smiled brightly. "I may read more of my novel, *Forever Amber*. That Kathleen Winsor is quite a clever writer, and maybe a bit on the *fun* side, too!"

Aunt Cora headed for the living room where we knew she kept her current book. Watching her go, Nat turned to me. "Why don't we go for a walk in the orchards? I kind of feel like getting some exercise on this nice spring day.

At first I didn't think she was serious, but she grabbed my arm and whispered, "*Come on!*"

I kept my voice low. "All right, Sis. But Walt Bunker's coming over this afternoon. We're gonna play some catch, and, you know, have a little fun doing guy stuff."

Her eyes turned bright. "Okay, then, let's not waste any time!"

Walking outside on the pleasant afternoon, we strolled toward the lane that winds around behind the barn. A few moments later she grinned. "Did you see Dad looking over the church secretary?"

"Well, yeah, I did." I glanced at her. "But, *so what*?"

"*James*! Didn't he look like he was a young man checking her out? I sure thought so."

"Hold on, Nat! If Dad wants to 'check out' a good-looking woman, well, I think he should. You don't think he's gonna stay a widower forever, do you?"

I studied her face as we passed the old pickup truck that I used to drive to the mountain cabin last summer in pursuit of Otto Herman and his companion Derek Miller. "After all, Sis, if Dad wants to get involved with another woman, we have to hope she will be a good wife, and, a good stepmother."

"Well … I kind of thought Dad was getting a little sweet on Aunt Cora."

Glancing up at a couple of robins that darted over us, I took a look at my sister. "That's not exactly our concern, is it? If you brought me out here to get me involved in some campaign to get rid of Missus LaSalle, forget it."

I had to smile. "I've got Linda, my own girlfriend, in case you haven't noticed."

"Okay, Big Brother. I get the idea. But before we go back, you must know that if Dad *does* get involved with another woman, it's going to affect our *entire household.*"

After a few more strides, she stopped. "Just suppose … suppose Dad is interested in Aunt Cora. Well, look at their ages. Dad's birthday is October 5, so he'll be 43 this year, and Cora, I think she's going to be 44 on September 1st. That's no *real difference,* is it?"

I frowned. "No, I guess you can say they're the same age …"

As I thought about their ages, Nat added, "Aunt Cora looks about like Mom. The black and white pictures in our family album don't do either one justice, but let's compare them. Mom was about five-foot-three, and Aunt Cora is maybe an inch taller. Otherwise, our aunt looks a lot like our mother used to look, and Mom certainly was attractive. Aunt Cora has the same brown hair, but a little shorter with flecks of gray. And not only that but she has the same brown eyes, maybe a bit larger, the same nice nose, the same thin lips, and the *works*!"

Nat grinned. "You know it's all true, James. I have to say that if Dad was searching for a wife who looked like our mother, he couldn't find a better match. While you're trying to think of why I'm wrong, here's my main point. Aunt Cora *knows us*, and we *know* her. Missus LaSalle might be a great person, but she would have to get to *know us*!"

I took a deep breath. "Think about this. Suppose Dad *does* want to get married again, and suppose he *does* look for another wife, and suppose all that stuff about Aunt Cora you said is true. Still, he's the one who has to make that choice, not us."

Nat's expression looked crestfallen, and I thought, *Uh-uh, now she needs a lift*. "Look, Sis. I'm just saying there's no rush. All these things may well come to pass, but I'm gonna lay low, work on the farm, and play baseball."

I nodded toward the house. "Let's head back. Dad's a level-headed guy, and he won't rush into anything. Pretty soon summer will be here, and I'm gonna have plenty of fun!"

"Okay, James, but just be aware … Dad may surprise us." After a few more steps, she added, "I'm going to have some fun too!" She grinned. "So we're even, Big Brother!"

We walked the rest of the way to the house. On the back porch Aunt Cora was sitting in a rocking chair with a bowl of potatoes, peeling them with a paring knife. Looking at her, I thought, *Actually, we're fortunate she's willing to live here with us. We will see what we see.*

III

Hearing an engine in the driveway, I checked my watch. It was 2:00. I descended the stairs and looked out the dining room window. Walt Bunker was climbing out of a shiny black 1940 Chevrolet with whitewall tires. I knew the Bunkers owned a '35 blue Chevy four-door. Walt washed that car every Saturday afternoon, hoping to be a regular driver after he turned 16. I forgot he'd celebrated his birthday in mid-January, so I thought, *Now he's driving too.*

I hurried outside to where he waited, grinning. "Hey, James! Check our new wheels! My dad bought this black 1940 Chevrolet Deluxe three days ago, and he gave me permission to drive it here today. Man, look at the finish on this black beauty!"

Rubbing his hand over the hood, he continued: "A teacher from Staunton put it up for sale a few days ago, and Dad saw the advertisement in the *Charlottesville Record*."

We stood and looked at the shiny four-door sedan while Walt talked about its sterling qualities like he was a salesman. "You know my Dad. He doesn't like to wait! So when he spotted the ad, he called the guy long-distance, wangled a price out of him, and promised he'd drive over by 11:00 am. He works as a plumber for the grounds crew at the university, but a colleague covered for him on Friday. He and Mom drove over to Staunton. They liked it, and they bought it."

He grinned. "Of course, Mom's gonna drive the old four-door, but when she doesn't want to drive that car, then I get it. Dad promised I could drive to school this spring and next fall for my senior year. Like the Bible says in Psalm 23, *"My cup runneth over."*

Marveling at the vehicle, I observed, "It does look almost *new*. You just washed it, right?"

We laughed, because we agreed. For another ten minutes we compared the features on the Bunkers' 1940 Chevrolet and the Bakers' 1939 Chevy, and there wasn't a lot of difference. We owned a blue Chevrolet Master Sedan, instead of the black Master model. Otherwise, both looked very modern, and they ran like tops. As we spoke, I stood there thinking, *Even farm boys like to talk cars, drive them, and feel like we're up-to-date with trends and styles.*

Walt retrieved his Spalding baseball glove and an old baseball from the back seat, and I got my Wilson southpaw's glove from the house. Last summer Dad also bought me a Rawlings trapper's mitt, because sometimes I play first base. But Walt had his fielder's glove, so I used mine. We walked out behind the barn to play catch. We must have tossed that scuffed baseball back and forth for half an hour. Stopping, Walt motioned me over.

Looking around, he lowered his voice. "Have you noticed how Wanda Winston has changed since last year? She's got that red hair, a few freckles, and those ocean blue eyes, but she is *filling out*, if you know what I mean. I think she's gonna look like another *Rita Hayworth*!"

I smiled, and he added, "Wanda's got real *nice legs*, too, and I do mean *nice*!"

"Holy cow, Walt! I can't think of the last time you made any sexy comments about girls!"

"Yeah, well, I guess she slipped past my x-ray eyes. But Wanda and your sister are buddies, aren't they?"

He lifted his eyebrows twice, and grinned, knowing I knew the sign for *Very Good Looking*.

We laughed, and he leaned closer. "So, last night you took Linda Lawton, and Herb took Iris Hofner to the movies, right? Well, they've gotta be two of the *coolest* sophomores at Jefferson."

Talking about girls beats practicing baseball, and Walt plunged ahead. "While you two guys were out painting the town, I got to take our old Chevy. So, I picked up Wanda, and took her to Sammy's. We had hamburgers and shakes, and we drove around town until dark. Then, see, I find a spot to park, but only *if* the girl is *with me*." He grinned crookedly. "Get it?"

I had to smile. "So, Walt, are you saying you got in a little *makin' out* last night?"

"You're thinking too far ahead, James, but I'm *hoping*. Anyway, once you've got that first serious date under the belt, we both know kissing the girl is on deck! Anyhow, don't say anything to your sister. She and Wanda are buddies, and we know the girls share 'guy stuff.' So if Wanda's ready next time, I can't wait!"

Walt's smile practically wrapped around his face. "Listen, maybe you and I can make some plans for a double date ourselves, maybe one weekend soon."

We smiled at each other. "*Hail to the weekend*" we chanted in unison. All of a sudden, we just broke out laughing. I took a second look at Walt, and I realized he's filling out too. About my height of 6'0", he has brown curly hair, wide brown eyes, and a slender build. But like me, he's already shaving. And now I can tell he's got better athletic skills and a stronger arm.

I grinned. "C'mon, Walt! Let's play high catch!"

We moved about twenty feet apart. Taking turns, each of us threw the ball as high as he could, and the other one had to judge the arc and move under the ball to make the catch, just like you do to field a popup or a fly ball in a game.

Walt went first, yelling, "Here you go, James!" He winged the ball higher than the top of a maple tree, and I looked up to judge it, but I had to run several feet to make the grab.

"All right, Walt, here goes!"

I flung one up just as high, and Walt circled a couple of times before making the catch. Retrieving it from his glove, he grinned. In a flash he threw another one even higher. The ball reached its peak, curved over, and zipped down like a diving eagle. Again I made a good catch. Bracing myself, I heaved one as high as I could.

We played high catch for about fifteen minutes, and I could tell we were getting tired. At that point, I yelled, "Last one!"

Each of us made one more throw and one more catch. Afterward, I smiled. "C'mon, let's go inside. Aunt Cora always has a jug of lemonade in the fridge. You'll like her lemonade!"

"Good 'ol James! You sure know how to call 'em. I can use one of your aunt's lemonades!"

We went past the Bunkers' car, Walt flipped his glove into the front seat, and I carried mine as we headed for the kitchen. Inside, I plopped my glove on the cabinet beside the back door. Dad, with the morning newspaper under his arm, stood peering into the fridge.

"Hey, Dad! Walt and I have been playing catch!"

He wheeled around and smiled. "I suppose you two are practicing your baseball skills on this nice Sunday afternoon, right!"

"Yes, sir, Mister Baker." Walt smiled. "How are you today, sir?"

Dad grinned. "Well, since you're good enough to ask, I'm about to stretch out on the couch with the Sunday *Record*. I just might doze off … you can never tell."

Winking, he walked toward the living room. When he reached the living room and sat down, Walt remarked, "Your Dad is one cool customer, James. Naturally, *I* know *you* know that!"

I grinned, and Walt noticed the wall clock. "You know what? I should get going. You never know when a guy needs to take his mom somewhere. Of course, you get more driving time, too!"

We walked outside together. Climbing in the car, Walt closed the door and started the engine. Got a minute or so we listened to the smooth sound of the six-cylinder. Looking up at me, Walt smiled. "See you tomorrow, James!"

"See you, Walt!" I watched the Chevy roll along the driveway. Honking, he turned toward town.

IV

I didn't see Natalia for the rest of Sunday afternoon because she kept busy in her bedroom. When we sat down at the kitchen table just before 6:00, the four of us bowed our heads and Dad offered his usual grace: "Our heavenly Father, we ask you to bless us, and to bless this food to its intended use. We offer thanks for your bounty, through Jesus, our Lord. Amen."

Aunt Cora had prepared meatloaf, green beans, fresh-baked cornbread, and instant coffee. For dessert a bowl of our Red Delicious apples sat on the table, and all four of us enjoyed one. After the meal, Nat announced that she was going upstairs to do more homework.

She headed for the staircase, and I watched her climb the steps. Aunt Cora gave me a knowing look like she and Nat had spent time together. I asked Dad what he planned to listen to on the radio. We had three radios upstairs, a Zenith that Dad gave me, a Philco that Nat received after Mom passed away, and an Emerson floor model that Cora brought when she moved here.

Dad's pride and joy was his Zenith Empire of Radio console that stands next to the living room couch. I've seen him polish its dark wood, and Nat and I listen to that radio with Dad and Aunt Cora every time President Roosevelt delivers a "Fireside Chat." One Saturday last spring Dad turned it on when Walt was visiting. Listening to its rich tones, my friend dubbed it the "Emperor," and we all laughed!

I climbed the staircase, and at the top I could hear soft music from Nat's room as Perry Como crooned "People Will Say We're in Love." Smiling, I went into my room, leaving the door ajar.

That popular song prompted me to stand in front of the mirror and look at my reflection. The music evoked a mental image of our attractive mother, but soon her face faded and Nat's face appeared. Maybe talking to my sister about the similarities of Mom and Aunt Cora started my mind working. Several pictures in our family album show that Nat looks like a younger version of our mother Mary, who was killed by a drunk driver in 1937.

Nat, who at 5'5" is a couple of inches taller than Mom was, has similar brown hair, but she wears a little longer these days. Her eyes look more greenish rather than the greenish-brown of our mother, but my sister has the same oval face, nice nose, and thin lips. The more I think about it, the more I realize Mom, Cora, and Nat look quite similar, and all three are very attractive.

Looking in the mirror again, I realize I look more like Dad when he was younger, kind of in the way that Nat looks more like Mom used to look. Dad is taller than me, but I reached six feet this spring. Otherwise, I have his blue eyes, brown hair, and suntanned skin and, I hope, a fair amount of his athletic ability. Guys like Coach Spencer in baseball and teammates like Walt, Herb Jenkowski, and Jack Jones think I'm a real good ballplayer, and that pleases me.

Since I began playing on school and summer teams at age ten, I usually play left field and first base, and I have the gloves for both positions. I bat right-handed, but I throw left-handed. Coach Spencer, who's a pretty smart guy, used to play baseball and football himself.

Of course, he's the head football and baseball coach at Jefferson. About my height, he's stocky with small blue eyes, close-cropped brown hair, and dimples on his cheeks. His voice is authoritative, and when he speaks, you listen.

This spring the coach wanted me to become a pitcher. I paid close attention when he showed me some pitching fundamentals such as gripping the ball, making the ball break, and completing the follow through. My speed isn't great, and I can bend a curve, but I call my best pitch a "drop ball." Any pitch depends on how you grip the ball, throw it, and spin it off your fingers. In the big leagues, I know some pitchers can hurl a slider. But my drop bends a little on the way, but the ball takes a quick dip at home plate.

A quiet knock interrupted my thoughts. Turning, I saw my sister smiling. "Can I come in, James?"

"Sure, Sis. I'm about to do some reading. Things are quiet downstairs. Dad and Aunt Cora are listening to the radio."

I sat on the side of my bed facing her, and Nat sat in the captain's chair at my rolltop desk facing me. My black alarm clock said 8:05. She looked thoughtful, and I waited more than a minute to hear what she had in mind. Getting up, I walked to my window and looked toward the empty spot where Otto Herman's house once stood. As I gazed at the fields, I felt Nat touch my arm.

"James, I didn't mean to bother you, but I've got stuff on my mind." She peered at me with her bright eyes. "What I'm going to tell you is strictly between us."

When I nodded, she said, "I helped Aunt Cora for a while in the kitchen, and I might have baked some good cornbread!"

I had to smile. "But I also learned certain personal information from Aunt Cora, and," she lowered her voice, "don't you *dare* tell anyone I repeated it!"

When I nodded, she whispered, "Cross your heart, and hope to die."

Now she wanted the time-worn kid's phrase for keeping a promise. "Look, Nat, we're in high school. I promise not to repeat it, but tell me. I've got reading to do."

Sighing, she relented. "Okay, here it is. Earlier we talked about Aunt Cora maybe having a boyfriend, you know, like Dad?" She focused on my eyes, waiting.

"Yes, I agree that can happen."

"Well, she's thinking about Dad, all right, but she confided that he's oblivious to her. That's her word, *oblivious*!" She rolled her eyes. "Before today, Aunt

Cora hadn't given me any indication she's thinking along romantic lines. But, brother, there's more!!"

She surprised me, but I kept listening. "You just took Aunt Cora to Jack's Grocery, correct?" When I nodded, she continued: "Did you see a tall man working there, sandy hair, blue eyes, kind of like that."

"Now that you mention it, that man spoke to Herb, who works part time there. I wouldn't be surprised if he's Jack Johnson, the owner, so he's the man in charge."

Nat's eyes twinkled. "Well, Aunt Cora *thinks* he's a 'good-looking' man with a solid position in life, and he's not married."

She grinned. "Events are moving faster than I thought, James. Do you think a little bird should sing a song to Dad before he loses his dinner?"

For several long seconds we looked at each other, and then we broke out laughing! When we finally stopped, Nat whispered, "Keep the secret."

Once again I smiled as he slipped out of my room.

Chapter 3

High School

After dinner on Monday evening, it might have been curiosity that pulled my eyes to the wall calendar next to the refrigerator. The date was April 19, and I filed it mentally. I sat there at the kitchen table sipping a glass of lemonade, relaxing, and watching my family members. I liked seeing Dad help Aunt Cora by drying the dishes after she washed them. Natalia also helped by putting the dishes and silverware away.

The last rays of the setting sun came in the back door, and I saw sunbeams dancing on the linoleum floor. Earlier, Dad pronounced the fried chicken "quite good," and Nat and I thought the dinner was one of Aunt Cora's best. Smiles lightened everyone's mood.

A loud knock came from the front door. Reacting, Nat hurried through the dining room and living room, trailed by Dad and Aunt Cora. Curious, I followed them. When Nat opened the door, I saw a familiar-looking young man about my height with sandy blonde hair, big shoulders, and a stocky build. He must have weighed close to 200 pounds. Looking nervous, he peered at us from his big brown eyes. When my sister greeted him cheerfully, he smiled.

"Hi, Nat," he said in a deep voice. "I hope you're not busy."

I didn't know his name, but I recognized him from Jefferson High. "Good evening, folks," he said, nodding. "I'm sorry if I have surprised you. My name is Henry Wolinski. I'm a senior at Jefferson, and …"

Dad stepped forward, extended his right hand, and gripped Henry's hand firmly. As he eyed our father with red rising in his cheeks, Dad asked, "What brings you to our house?"

Nat came to his rescue. "Dad, Henry's *my friend*. He played center on Jefferson's football team last fall, and his application is pending at the University of Virginia. His father runs Wolinski Clothiers, you know, the shop downtown. I told him he could stop by our house when we finished our homework, and I think Henry has a *book* for me."

Dad grinned. "Well, then, Henry. Come in and meet our family. Evidently you know my daughter Natalia." Indicating our aunt, he said, "This is Cora, my sister-in-law, and I imagine you know James, my son."

Henry's eyes said he recognized me, and he bowed to Aunt Cora. Looking relieved, he turned to Dad. "Well, sir, I don't have much time this evening, but your daughter is writing a paper on Monticello, and I can help her because we're researching and writing term papers for Senior English, and I happen to be doing mine about Monticello."

Now he seemed at ease. "Thomas Jefferson designed the home, and over the years he redesigned it, using neoclassical architecture that he learned from his own reading and travel experiences. Monticello is filled with many of Jefferson's inventions that were used to make life go more smoothly, and I've read up on those, too. So … Monticello is a *fascinating* place to visit."

Dad smiled. "Yes, we saw it once, but I have to say that was several years ago."

As I listened to this impromptu lecture, I noticed Dad was taking it in stride, but Nat looked like she wanted to drop through a hole in the floor. To help her, I switched the topic.

"Henry, I saw you playing on offense and defense on the line at our football games last fall, and our team's linemen are strong guys who played well all season. What got you interested in playing football?"

Again he smiled. "I've been helping the football team at my position, but I'm a senior, so football is over for me. My favorite sport is baseball. But Dad runs the shop, and I handle the work on the farm. I don't have time for baseball, even though I really like playing the game."

I nodded. "I was just curious, because I like football too. But like you, I've got plenty to do on the farm, so I stick to one sport, and for me it's baseball."

Henry interjected: "Actually, James, I saw you play baseball last year with the JVs, but so far this year I haven't been able to make it to a varsity game. But you have *excellent* hand-eye coordination, and Jack Jones, one of my friends, says you're a fine athlete."

I felt the color rising in my cheeks. "Well, that's pretty nice of you to say, Henry, but I've seen you play football, and I know you're an outstanding athlete. Anyway, it's nice to meet you."

I stepped forward, and we shook hands, and Dad asked, "Where is your family's farm, Henry?"

Hoisting his right thumb over his shoulder, he replied, "We live a mile east of here, and about two miles southeast of town. My father owns a 100-acre farm. We grow an acre of Albemarle Pippins, but mainly we raise wheat, oats, and rye, plus we have a garden."

He smiled. "I guess these days we're calling them 'Victory Gardens'!"

Glancing at his silver wrist watch, he said, "I do need to get rolling. I have more reading to do for American Literature."

Nat smiled brightly. "I'll walk with you to the car. I'm interested in what you're learning about Monticello."

"That's nice," Henry remarked. Pulling a 3x5 note card from his shirt pocket, he handed it to her. "Check this book at the school library. It's Thomas S. Randall's *Life of Thomas Jefferson*, first published in 1857. The book will probably help with your Monticello paper."

Not to be left out, Aunt Cora added her personal touch. "I enjoyed meeting you, Henry, and I do hope you'll come back and see us again."

Henry nodded, Nat grabbed his hand, and they strolled toward the car. He had arrived in a blue 1938 Dodge sedan with a dented right front fender. Watching them walk away, I smiled. Henry got off on the wrong foot, but he redeemed himself. On the other hand, I wondered how Nat became involved with a senior, especially a guy that I'd never even heard her mention.

Ready to go up to my room, I looked outside. I could see the sun setting over the orchards. While I was gazing toward the sinking orange ball, it occurred to me a better question might be what got Henry interested in Nat. I chuckled, because I'll probably hear the answer soon enough.

II

I arrived at school with my duffel bag and a couple of books on Tuesday morning about 8:15. Like other teenagers who were allowed to drive, I parked in the lot behind Jefferson High on Main Street. One side was reserved for teachers, and that side was next to the rear wall. Other school employees parked there too, but not the public. Every now and then Burt

Blackstone, the patrol officer, would leave a "ticket" on the windshield of a car not displaying the school ID. I heard there's no fine involved, so nobody cares much about being ticketed.

The important point for drivers is to arrive early enough to find a parking place. If you arrive after 8:20, you may have to look on a street close to the school. Actually, during the war years, I guess a larger problem is whether you have enough money and coupons to buy rationed gas.

Carrying my duffel bag and books in the back entrance, I spotted Linda Lawton. She was hanging out on the far side of the hall near the library door and talking to a couple of girls. I said *Hi*, and she gave me a big smile. Stepping forward, I asked how she liked *Casablanca*. Her reply was, "I *loved i*t!"

Coming closer, she said, "I hope you can pick out another good movie pretty soon!"

Catching me off guard, she looked into my eyes, made a kissing gesture with her lips, and turned back to her girlfriends. As I walked away, I could hear the girls talking about me, and that means I made a hit!

Walking up the stairs, I headed to room 201, which faces the playground and athletic fields. Home Room, as we call it, is a 25-minute "class" where the eleventh graders gather in the morning for various purposes, including school news for the day. In fact, all four of the high school grades start the day with Home Room.

First I went to my locker, put my baseball stuff inside, selected my books and notebooks for morning classes, and spoke to some friends. A couple minutes later, I walked into room 201 and to my assigned desk in the row next to the windows. The big event coming up is the Senior Prom, but that's already planned.

Once you're in the ninth grade, you can go to the Prom, so it's not reserved for seniors. But the dance honors the senior class, and most of the teachers serve as chaperones. I've never had a "steady" girlfriend, so if I can get Linda to go, this will be my first year. Anyway, there was no other business, so Coach Jackson took the roll, and after that we sat and spent the time talking with friends sitting nearby.

The bell rang at 8:55, and everyone got up and headed for 9:00 classes. Mine was US History that Mister Bronston was teaching in room 205, two doors away. In the hallway I heard guys and girls making the typical teen comments like "What's up with you?" "How'd you do on the test?," and "What are you doing this weekend?" School corridors are always busy between classes, and plenty of plans are made in such hurry-up circumstances.

Once in Mister Bronston's room, I went to my desk in the second row. While others were getting seated, I put my books on the right side, opened my spiral notebook, and took out a pencil. When the bell rang, the round clock on the front wall above the blackboard showed it was exactly 9:00, and the chatter faded.

Mister Bronston, a man about my height with thinning black hair, quick-moving dark eyes, and a steady voice, stood behind the teacher's desk tapping the eraser end of his pencil on the desktop The pencil-tapping is a sign he's ready to begin, and he dislikes anyone showing up late. In fact, a latecomer risks a negative crack about his or her behavior in future life.

When the last student was seated, Bronston took the roll, looking where each person was sitting and putting a check by that name in the gradebook. Closing the book, he launched into his lecture. Last week we covered the major events of World War II. Already we finished the textbook, but it only covers up to the League of Nations and the year 1920. Since then, Bronston has been talking about interesting parts of the war, and he brings in newspaper clippings or letters from friends or relatives who are involved in the war, at home or overseas.

Last week we covered rationing because everyone's family is affected. Families like ours living on farms have fewer problems getting the necessary food, but people living in towns and cities are expected to grow "Victory Gardens." Anything less is considered unpatriotic, and I'm sure the people seen as unpatriotic are criticized.

Today Bronston showed us copies of a letter that he received from a nephew who lives near St. John's, Newfoundland. Bronston knows quite a bit about Newfoundland, Canada's easternmost province, thanks to letters from his brother-in-law and the nephew. This particular letter covered the experiences of the nephew who works as a mechanic in the Royal Canadian Air Force. We learned the Canadians are sending up B-24 Liberator Bombers from Torbay, an airport north of St. John's, to track German submarines in the North Atlantic. The nephew's best friend is a co-pilot. His B-24 sank a U-boat last year, but a government censor redacted any identifying details. The friend told Bronston's nephew about seeing a Navy Coast Guard cutter picking up three German seamen, who jumped from their sub before the crew scuttled it.

Mister Bronston answered a few questions, but Jimmy Wilson, usually a smart aleck who doesn't pay much attention, asked what the Coast Guard did with the Germans who abandoned the sub.

"I thought we're supposed to be killing these guys," Jimmy said. "Why didn't they just let 'em drown?"

"You can't do that," Bronston shot back. "If you don't follow basic fair play rules in a war, all sides will start doing the same deadly stuff." When Jimmy smirked and shook his head, Bronston replied with the evil-eye. He asked, "Suppose you're drafted into the armed forces and you end up on a Navy ship. Do you want to be left to drown if something goes wrong with *your* ship?"

Jimmy's face turned red as a beet, and he said nothing else, but in a few minutes the 9:55 bell rang. I think everyone felt relieved to leave the difficult situation and go to their next class. I guess some people think Americans ought to brutalize German soldiers or sailors or let them die, but Bronston was telling us, in effect, it's always different when the shoe's on your foot.

When the 10:00 bell rang, I was sitting at my first row desk in Miss DeRoche's English class. Walt Bunker sits in the desk behind me, and Herb Jenkowski sits behind Walt. Both of them like hearing my ideas for better writing, and of course we're baseball buddies. Miss DeRoche always calls the roll, and she did it today.

Like most of our female teachers, she arrives at school dressed neatly in a black, brown, or blue skirt and a white or light-colored blouse and flat shoes. A blue-eyed blonde who styles her hair in the Victory Roll, the way she smiles, talks, and appears catches your eye, at least for the guys.

Miss DeRoche covered infinitives again, and we all took a turn using an infinitive in a sentence that we wrote on the blackboard. When the class ended, the main point seemed to be not to "split infinitives." I noticed most of the girls already understood that concept, but several guys like Herb and Walt and Jack Jones usually have questions. I caught on pretty quick, and hopefully one day I'll be skilled enough to be a good author.

After English class, I headed for my study hall at 11:00, Herb went to American Literature, and Walt had Geography. For Miss DeRoche's homework, we have to write a one-page essay on a "home front" topic that US families are facing during the war, and, naturally we can't split infinities. I'm going to write about automobile sales, because I hope to buy a used car.

Like most guys, I'd rather show up at a girl's house in a vehicle I can call "my car." Of course, during the war you need coupons to buy gas, but that won't always be the case. Also, the military uses the railroads to transport troops from one Army or Navy base to another, so civilians have a tougher time getting tickets on trains. I was mulling over those thoughts and working on my essay when the period ended at 11:55. Collecting my books and notebooks, I headed to the cafeteria.

I saw Nat seated in one corner of the large room filled with rows of tables and metal chairs. She was sitting next to Wanda Winston. Wanda stands out because of her red hair, and she's a sophomore like Nat. My sister told me she and Wanda have three classes together. One of them is World History, and tenth graders take it from Mister Bronston.

 When I looked at Wanda, I remembered Walt hinting about his date with her last Saturday evening and his hopes for the next date. I figure Wanda was sharing her dating experience with Nat, more or less like boys share their experiences with friends.

Herb Jenkowski waved at me from a table where mostly juniors sit. It's funny how high school kids tend to stick together by grades, almost like cliques. A bigger deal is that guys or girls on a team or in a club will sit together. Maybe it's the "birds of a feather" principle. I think everyone likes talking to a friend, neighbor, or classmate when you're eating lunch, sitting at a game, or whatever.

Picking up a tray, I moved into the lunch line, and in no time I had a chicken drumstick, a scoop of mashed potatoes, a portion of peas, and a peach. I went over and sat next to Herb, who was talking with Jack Jones, sitting on the opposite side of the table. Jack is one of our best outfielders, and he's always one of the first four hitters. He's another lean, muscled, and strong athletic type like Herb. Jack has blue eyes, blonde hair, quick reflexes, and a solid knowledge of the game. His family lives over on Preston Avenue in one of those stylish two-story houses. He and Herb were talking about movies for the coming weekend.

"Hey, James," Jack said between bites of an apple. "What're you up to, buddy?"

Herb interrupted. "Get this, Jack. Me and James took our girls to see *Casablanca* on Saturday. We had *heavy* dates, and we both drove. The movie, well, it's *great*. I could see that one again. But afterward, I don't know about James because he's close-mouthed. But I had a swell time, buddy. Girls like seeing those dramatic movies. I think it makes 'em feel like kissing guys, but you need to be smart and not get, you know, *pushy*."

Jack was grinning. "Yeah, I saw that Bogart movie two Saturdays ago when I took Claudia Rogers. I'll tell you she's one *cute* girl. I love seeing her pretty face, hazel eyes, and long wavy brown hair. She's sort of a bookworm, you know, but very attractive, nice to be with, but a little shy. She does *love* a good movie, and get this: it doesn't even have to be a romance!"

We smiled at Jack, and he winked at us. Leaning forward, he lowered his voice. "I don't think Claudia goes in much for making out, but I'll kiss her in the next movie!"

I interjected. "You both know we're playing Lee High at home this Friday afternoon, right?"

"Yeah, we'll take hitting and infield today," replied Herb. "I hear Lee's got two senior outfielders who have a real shot at college baseball. This is gonna be a tough game."

That shifted the talk away from girls and back to baseball, causing Jack and Herb to retell some of the adventures from various games. I listened, ate, and added a few comments.

After lunch I had my three afternoon classes, Geometry, Geography, and Phys Ed, and all three went smooth. I hurried to my locker, grabbed my baseball duffel bag, and made it to the locker room at 3:10. Before changing for baseball practice, I felt like swigging a bottle of soda. The coach insists the school keep a Coca-Cola machine outside the locker room.

When I got there, the Shenandoah Soda company's driver was restocking the bottles. I pulled out a nickel, and he grinned. Taking my coin, he handed me a bottle. I popped the cap on the machine's opener. A few of the guys who arrived earlier were drinking Cokes and telling guy jokes and laughing. I sat down with them and joined in.

III

On Wednesday around 6:00, we sat down to eat dinner with Aunt Cora. Today she fixed pork chops, cauliflower, peas, and more cornbread. Dad wasn't home for dinner, which is unusual. When Nat asked, Aunt Cora said airily, "He went on a *date*."

My sister stared at our aunt for several long seconds. Finally, she observed, "You're telling us Dad's gone out with Missus LaSalle, right?"

"Well … Yes, I *believe* he has taken Missus LaSalle to dinner, but he didn't say so, not in *those words*." She sighed. "But that would be my guess."

Nat rolled her eyes. "A pretty good guess, though, given what we know."

"Yes," Cora replied, cutting her pork chop into small pieces. "It's probably *more* than a guess."

Gazing at both of us, Aunt Cora tried to look deadpan, but I could see the hurt in her eyes. I'm sure Nat picked up on it too. Glancing at me, my sister turned to eating her pork chop. I took it as her signal to drop the subject. If Aunt Cora wanted to talk about it, she would have to start the conversation. Even so, you can hardly talk to your father about his love life.

After we finished eating, Nat helped Aunt Cora clear the dishes and I headed for the barn to groom the two horses. Lady, the brown mare, is 21, and Midnight, the black quarter horse, is 22, so both of them are getting along in years. They're kind of like large friendly pets, but we do ride them a couple of times a week. However, these days we never ride either horse hard.

By the time I finished with the horses, the sun had dipped below the horizon. Still, the western sky was glowing brightly with a kaleidoscope of orange, yellow, and red. Closing the barn door, I headed toward the back porch. At the porch I stopped and looked around. Dusk was filtering into the air. When you visualize it, nightfall looks like a motion picture where millions of black dots slowly but steadily assemble into an ever darker blanket that engulfs the world.

As I gazed at the darkening sky, a brown barn owl swooped low near me and dug its talons into a rodent scurrying across the yard. I heard a *whoosh*, a tiny squeak, and the flapping of long wings as the owl rose like a feathered flying machine. I watched it land on the bottom limb of the oak in our side yard. Facing me, the owl ruffled its wings. The two tufts on top of its head looked like a pair of ears. The bird seemed to stare at me, and I just turned and went inside.

About that time I heard the familiar sound of our Chevrolet's motor in the driveway. I looked out a kitchen window as Dad parked. Aunt Cora and Nat heard the engine too, because they appeared in the kitchen seconds later. Cora moved to the counter, glanced out, and began placing the washed dishes into the cupboard. I smiled to myself, realizing she probably saved that little task for this purpose. Nat looked at me, and mouthed *I'm going to ask him.*

Suddenly I felt like a fifth wheel. I was curious too, but I realized Nat would tell me whatever Dad said. Grinning, I went into the dining room and headed up the stairs, two at a time. In my bedroom I sank onto the wooden chair at my rolltop desk. My school books were stacked on the right, and I thought, *No time like the present to finish my essay for Miss DeRoche.* I could hear voices floating up to the second level, but I couldn't make out the words.

Fifteen minutes later Nat appeared in my doorway, and I turned to face her. "Guess what?" She sounded breathless. "Dad *did* take Missus LaSalle out to dinner, and at Harry's Fine Food. When I asked how it went, he said the place was fancy. When I pressed him, he indicated he liked the food, but he said, quote, It can never match what your Aunt Cora cooks, unquote."

Nat grinned. "Aunt Cora was listening from the sink, and when Dad said that, she turned and looked at him as if she couldn't believe her ears! I could hardly believe mine either, but I tried to hide my surprise. In a minute or so, Aunt Cora asked, 'Did the two of you have a nice time?'

"Dad said they did have a nice time,' and he really liked the turkey dinners they ordered. He said the service was good, the food was good, and they talked about their families. I gather Missus LaSalle gave him some background from her earlier years. After a while they ordered dessert, which was strawberry pie. Well, it *sounds* like a good time to me."

As my sister continued with her news, I listened and thought it over. "I hope Dad told you more about the evening. What you've said sounds pretty ordinary, like 'We went out to eat, we had a turkey dinner, and we had a good time.' Isn't there *more*?"

Nat's big smile flashed like a neon sign. "There you go, Big Brother. Let's see what you think. Her first name is Helen, her little girl's name is Joyce, and she's six, but we knew all that. Dad also said Helen grew up in Roanoke, graduated from a high school named Monroe, worked as a waitress after graduation, and married a guy named Ralph Beverly, who's also from Roanoke. They were married three years, she had the baby, and a couple of weeks after the kid was born, he left her. She struggled with babysitters and part-time jobs, until she got a break. She landed the church secretary's position, partly because the minister sympathized with her."

Nat's eyes smiled at me. "Of course, I realize this is all *secondhand*. But Dad also told me that several weeks after the husband deserted her and the child, the minister in Roanoke referred her to a minister in Charlottesville, Charles Benjamin, and as you know, he's the minister at our church. Helen came to town for a fresh start, but I think her story has holes in it. First, why did the husband leave? Second, if you want a 'fresh start,' why not move *farther away*? I doubt if Dad thinks he's heard the whole truth. He repeated how they had a nice time, but to me it sounds like he might be having second thoughts about Missus LaSalle."

Plopping down on the side of my bed, Nat faced me. "I was hoping to hear more, but maybe there's no more to hear. If you're wondering what we *don't know*, well, I'm wondering too."

We sat in silence for a couple of minutes, both thinking about our father and him meeting Missus LaSalle. To me the woman is good-looking with her blue eyes, black hair, charming face, and shapely figure. Still, I'm sure it will take more than good looks to impress Dad.

I smiled. "Anyhow, Nat, I'm glad you took time to inquire and listen. I felt like leaving because I was afraid if I asked questions too, it would seem like an *interrogation*."

Both of us stood up, and, all of a sudden, we hugged each other. I could feel Nat trembling, and I think fear of the unknown was causing each of us to be kind of nervous. Still, we both realize our lives are likely to change in ways that are beyond our control.

Chapter 4

Baseball, Natalia, and Surprises

Following our classes on Thursday, we would have baseball practice. Like the other guys, I was thinking about tomorrow's season opener against Staunton's Lee High. Classes end at 3:00. By the time we hurried to the locker room, changed clothes and put on tee shirts, sweatpants, baseball spikes, and trotted out to the diamond behind the school, it was about 3:30. Everyone knows Coach Spencer expects us to be changed and loosened up by that time. As usual, he waved for us to sit on the green wooden bleachers behind third base.

After we clambered onto the old bleachers in our spikes, the coach spoke for several minutes about the day's activities. Afterward, he clapped his, saying, "Let's go, guys!"

Climbing off the bleachers, we hit the field. The practice started with Coach Spencer hitting grounders to the infielders, and Coach Jackson hitting fly balls to the outfielders.

After the warmups, we took batting practice, with each of us getting maybe 5-6 swings. Coach Spencer always throws pregame BP on the day before game day. Jackson handles it on Mondays, and on other days our pitchers take turns throwing to several batters each.

After all of us took our swings under the coach's watchful eye, we played a game with eight guys plus the pitcher in the field, and the rest of the guys batting and running the bases until they racked up three outs. Today the hitting team played two "innings," Spencer made changes in the fielders, the pitcher, and the batters, and we played another two-inning "game." Practice normally lasts an hour and a half to an hour and three-quarters, and sometimes we just keep going until the coach is satisfied.

Today's practice was shorter, because Coach Spencer is satisfied that we're ready to go. Following a shower, drying off, and pulling on my school clothes, I waited a couple of minutes for Walt Bunker. We left the locker room about 4:45. I drove to school in the pickup today, so I dropped Walt off at his house, waved goodbye, and headed home. By the time I parked and walked into the kitchen, it was shortly after 5:00. To my surprise, Dad, Aunt Cora, and Natalia were sitting at the kitchen table. Dad and Cora were relaxing with coffee, and Nat was enjoying lemonade.

Setting my glove and duffel bag in the corner, I looked at Dad. He smiled. "You look like you're having a good day, James. How did baseball practice go?"

I grinned. "Yeah, we had a good practice." He didn't reply. Wondering what was up, I kept my eyes on Dad. "Am I late for something? I'm not aware of anything I forgot to do …"

"No problem, son. I just wanted Cora and Nat and you to know about a purchase I've made." He indicated an open chair. "Sit down for a few minutes."

I pulled up the chair. Dad was sitting at the far end of the table with an object wrapped in blue cloth lying in front of him. Aunt Cora sat to his left, and Nat to his right. I looked at them, and Dad cleared his throat. "We know what happened last spring when our neighbor and his young sidekick turned out to be secret Nazis. When Otto felt threatened, they kidnapped Natalia and Karl Ellis, Otto's nephew, supposedly to protect themselves from the FBI."

Dad sipped coffee. "In the end, Karl and Otto were both killed. On the way home, it seemed useful to give my Smith and Wesson .38 revolver to James' new friend Cecil, the son of the man who owns the country store called Elmer's Emporium. We owed that young man for directing the FBI to the out-of-the-way cabin where Nat and Karl were being held."

Dad paused, maybe to increase the impact. "What I want to tell you, and Cora and your sister already know, is that I purchased a .38 Colt Commando revolver from a friend in town. This gun," and he removed the cloth from around the weapon. "This six-shot revolver is the same caliber as the S&W we gave Cecil. But the more I think about it, the more I believe we need a gun, at least as long as World War II lasts."

He looked at us in turn. "I plan to keep it wrapped in this cloth and hidden in the kitchen." He pointed to the third drawer of the counter beside the refrigerator. "We will keep it in that drawer along with the clean dish cloths and dish towels."

He took a deep breath. "Cora, why don't you tell us what you think?"

Aunt Cora, looking a bit flustered, composed herself. "Well, since you ask … I really don't like having guns around the house. But I'm glad you're asking me, and I agree with owning the gun during *wartime*. But Zeke, if you expect me to shoot it, you need to show me *how*."

Cora wiped her forehead with a white handkerchief, sighing as if her statement took a load off her mind. Nodding, Dad turned inquiring eyes on Nat and me.

"I never would have thought I could shoot a pistol," my sister said quietly, "at least not before what happened last year. Well, I could use some training too."

Glancing at our aunt, she winked. "I can't have Aunt Cora *out-shooting* me, can I?!"

Dad chuckled. "Nat, I don't want you to feel pressured. If you really *don't* want to do this, I will understand if you just stay here."

Hesitating briefly, Nat looked at Dad. "No, I *want* to do it."

Dad turned to me, and I nodded. "Okay," he said, standing up. "Let's go out behind the barn and have a lesson."

He picked up the gun and walked out the kitchen door as Aunt Cora watched. Looking at us, she rolled her eyes, but she stood up and followed him without a word. Nat and I got up and went after them. We walked around behind the barn to a spot Dad had already set up for the purpose. I looked at a pile of hay bales, three high and two deep, a large padded target with its yellow bullseye and concentric rings of red, blue, and black. *So*, I thought, *he knew we were all going to agree, even with target practice.*

Dad checked the cylinder to make sure the Colt was loaded. Clicking it closed, he stepped up to a small board about twenty feet from the target. Eying Aunt Cora, he said, "Watch me." He closed the fingers of his right hand around the wooden grip, slowly elevated his arm, aimed with his right eye sighting along the barrel, and squeezed the trigger. The loud *bang* startled several pigeons in a nearby tree, and the beating of their wings signaled a mass retreat as the birds flew toward the orchard. Looking at the target, I saw a small hole in the right side of the red circle.

Dad smiled. Aiming again, he fired a second shot. Another *bang* sounded, and our horses whinnied inside the barn. A second hole had appeared, this one in the bottom of the red circle.

He handed the gun to Cora, who looked at it like she was holding a foreign object that fell from the moon. Her brown eyes opened wider as she looked at Dad. He smiled kindly, wrapped her right hand around the grip, and said, "Aim *carefully*, and squeeze the trigger *slowly*."

She complied, but I saw her close her eyes. Regardless, the loud bang followed, but I couldn't see a hole in the target. Unfazed, Dad smiled. "Try again, Cora," and he steadied her right arm with his right hand. "This time," he added smoothly, "try to keep your *right* eye open."

Nat smiled at me, but her expression turned deadpan. Again Cora aimed, and she squeezed the trigger, and in the instant after the bang, a hole appeared on the top right of the black circle.

Removing his hand, Dad said quietly, "Well done, Cora. Now fire two more shots."

Looking determined, she said, "I'm going to try both hands."

Facing the target, she raised the gun with both hands, and fired twice in quick succession. This time two holes appeared, one on the right of the black ring and another on the right of the blue ring.

Smiling, Dad said, "I'm impressed." He touched her arm. "Here, let me reload the revolver."

Aunt Cora released the gun like it was a hot coal she picked up by mistake, and the awed look on her face seemed almost comical. Nat eyed me, but we didn't speak as Dad pulled six cartridges from his pants pocket and reloaded the gun. Closing the cylinder, he motioned to Nat.

She stepped up to the board and took the revolver. First, she examined it like the gun made her suspicious. After glancing at Dad, she readied herself, aimed, squeezed off one shot, paused, fired again, paused, and fired a third time. We saw three holes in the red ring. Looking at the Colt, she blew the tiny spiral of smoke rising from the barrel like cowboys do in the movies.

I stifled a smile, thinking, *My sister is the heroine again, just like last year when she shot Otto, after he wounded me.*

Dad took the weapon from her, opened the cylinder, dug three cartridges from his pocket, reloaded it, and snapped the cylinder closed. "Here you go, James." He smiled and winked. "Go ahead and show us your stuff."

I moved over and stood just behind the board. Gripping the Colt in my left hand, I aimed carefully and shot once, twice, three times. One hole appeared in the yellow circle, two in the red circle, and it seemed like the barnyard kept echoing from the shots fired. This time we heard both horses snorting, stamping, and whinnying, but in a few moments they calmed down.

I handed the weapon back to Dad. "This Colt has a nice feel." I paused. "But, hopefully, we won't need to shoot at someone."

"Good enough," Dad replied, and he smiled. "Why don't we go back inside and have some of Cora's refreshments?"

"Yes, Zeke," and Aunt Cora was smiling. "I'll make *all* the refreshments you want!"

Dad pocketed the revolver, took her hand, and I watched the two walk hand-in-hand toward the house. Nat and I smiled as we trailed after them. I thought, *This is a surprise, for sure.*

II

I hate to admit it, but all day Friday I had to make myself focus on school work because my thoughts kept wandering back to baseball. I think almost everyone at Jefferson High knew the Lee High team would arrive this afternoon for the baseball opener. The first game is a pretty big deal, almost as big as our first football game in the fall. For me, this game was my first on the varsity, after playing two seasons of JV ball. I spoke to a few guys in the halls, and I know Herb, Jack, Walt, Damon Vann, and Scott Matthews, our newest player, were excited about the game.

In the locker room a few minutes after 3:00, Coach Spencer gave each of us a gray wool uniform with *Jefferson* printed in blue letters across the chest of the button-up jersey. Earning a varsity uniform makes you feel like you're part of something larger than a team, because you feel a sense of school pride and personal pride. Coach Jackson was handing everyone a white baseball undershirt with long blue sleeves, a blue ball cap with an orange letter J sewn to it, and a pair of blue high baseball socks with stirrups.

While Coach Jackson handed out the gear, Coach Spencer was walking back and forth, grinning and making comments to everyone. You could see the glow of pride in his eyes too. Already he had thumb tacked the lineup page on the bulletin board. After pulling on my uniform and my gear, I went over to take a look. I figured I would start, but I wanted to make sure.

Spencer's starting lineup read:

Jack Jones, LF
Scott Matthews, 3B
James Baker, 1B

Herb Jenkowski, C
Walt Bunker, P
Dave Pankavich, CF
Damon Vann, SS
Andy Thornton, 2B
Bob James, RF

That left Coach Spencer with three reserves: Matt Richards, a quiet junior who pitches and plays the outfield, Rob Henry, a lanky sophomore who can sub in the infield and pitch, and John Kilpatrick, a speedy sophomore who bats left-handed and is new this year to Jefferson baseball. I'm the only left-handed pitcher on the team, Jones and Kilpatrick are the only left-handed batters, and Vann and Pankavich are the only seniors.

While we donned uniforms, I could hear Coach Spencer talking quietly to Coach Jackson, probably about how to best use the starters as well as the subs. Ray Riley showed up and reported about using the school tractor to drag the infield. He also said the students and some parents were filling the bleachers on the home side. Lee had arrived with one school bus for players and another bus for students, and they were sitting behind the visitor's bench on the first base side.

I noticed Herb talking to Dave Pankavich, our center fielder. Dave is pretty good, especially in the field, but like many of us, he can use more self-confidence. I figured Herb was pumping him up, because I saw Dave smiling and nodding.

Actually, Herb has been the team leader since JV baseball back in the ninth grade. He knows his stuff, especially about baseball, and he's a star as well as the captain. In our sophomore year, Coach Spencer moved him to the varsity.

In football Herb plays fullback on offense and middle guard on defense, and he made the varsity as a two-way starter in the ninth grade. Nobody messes with Herb, certainly not at Jefferson. When I looked again, I saw him sitting by Scott, the new guy who moved here with his family last fall from Michigan. Herb was speaking quietly to him, and Scott was grinning.

Promptly at 3:40, Coach Spencer told us to sit on the side bench in front of the big mirror. After giving us final instructions, he waved us out to the diamond. We moved gingerly across the concrete locker room floor in our spiked shoes. Outside, we trotted across the playground to make what we call the team "entrance" through the gate onto our fenced-in baseball field.

The *entrance* is a Jefferson tradition, and all the guys look forward to it. I imagine the girls on our field hockey, basketball, and softball teams love the entrance too. When we enter, the people in the bleachers stand up and cheer, and it's inspiring. That is one of the many "highs" you get from playing on a team, for example, like singing the National Anthem before a football game.

In a few minutes the two teams had warmed up, and Jefferson's guys ran out on the field. Walt, our pitcher, threw a few warmup pitches, and he was ready. The coaches exchanged lineups, and two of our teachers, Mister Bronston and Mister Blackstone, the physics teacher, took the field in their bright blue umpire shirts and pressed gray slacks. They met at home plate with the coaches and captains to cover the ground rules. Afterward, Mister Bronston yelled, "Play Ball!"

Bronston took his position behind the catcher wearing his mask and chest protector, and Mister Blackstone stood back of first base. Once a team had one or more base runners, Mister Blackstone would move behind the pitcher for a better view.

Walt looked nervous, and even though Herb took a timeout to calm him, he walked the first two batters. With runners on first and second, one of the first of Lee's two really good seniors came up. Later, Herb mentioned his name, "Big Bill" McKinley, and he did look tall and strong.

McKinley took Walt's fastball outside for ball one, and he looked at a curveball that was low for ball two. Herb must have called for it, but Walt delivered a fastball about waist-high, and everyone heard the *crack* of the bat as McKinley lined the ball deep to center field. By the time Dave Pankavich could run down the ball in the back corner of the chain link fence in deep center and throw it to the infield, McKinley had rounded third, but he stopped and returned to the base.

The next batter was their other swell senior, and Herb later said his name is Phil Moorbridge. Oddly, the guy had the same stocky build as Herb, and Moorbridge proved to be a really good hitter. Walt missed outside with a fastball for ball one, and he followed with a waist-high curve ball, and *crack*! Moorbridge lifted a high fly ball that carried over the left field fence. All of a sudden, Jefferson trailed, 4-0, and we hadn't even batted in the first inning!

Coach Spencer left Walt in, but I swear his knees were shaking when the inning ended with Lee High ahead, 6-0. Between innings, the coach told Matt Richards to warm up in foul territory behind third base. It wasn't Walt's day, but seeing Matt getting loose gave us hope.

In the bottom of the first, Jack Jones, our left-handed batting long ball hitter, surprised their right-handed junior, Hank Butterfield, by blasting the first fastball for a long double to right center. With Jack grinning and taking a lead off second, Scott Matthews fouled off a couple of fast ones before he belted a long fly to right center. I was on deck, and the guys on the bench were on their feet and yelling, but Matthews' ball was caught. Still, Jones tagged up and trotted over to third.

Stepping up to bat, I took my stance, holding the bat low over my right shoulder.

From the stretch position, Butterfield threw two fastballs below the knees and one over the outside corner of the plate, which I took for a count of 2 balls and 1 strike. Butterfield threw me a good curve, but it broke just below the waist, and I drilled a single over second base. My hit allowed Jones to score from third with our first run, and that fired up the Jefferson fans on the third base side. Most of them began clapping, yelling, cheering, and stomping their feet on the wooden bleachers!

Standing on first, I glanced at the crowd. I saw Nat and Wanda cheering, and it gave me a buzz. Beside them sat Linda Lawton and Iris Hofner, and they looked excited too. Herb came up to bat fourth, or cleanup, and he just *looks* like a threat. He took a curveball down the middle like he had misjudged it. Butterfield, who might have been fooled when Herb took the pitch, delivered a second curveball in the same place.

Herb swung his bat so hard the loud *crack* when he connected sounded like two pieces of metal banged together! The ball rose on a majestic arc into deep left center, and it carried well beyond the chain link fence! The runners hustled around the bases and touched home plate, making the score Lee 6, Jefferson 3. Now the fans were really making a racket!

To make a long story short, the score see-sawed through six innings. Lee High would score a run or two off Matt's various curveballs, and Jefferson would come back and score a run or two off Butterfield's assorted offerings. Partly due to six walks by Matt, we still trailed in the sixth, 11-9, after Lee scored once in the top of the inning.

In the top half of the sixth, I made one nice play when their third baseman hit a hard bouncer up the middle that looked like a base hit. We had two outs, so the runner at second took off as soon as the hitter swung, but Andy "Scooter" Thornton, our slick-fielding second baseman, was playing the right-handed batter closer than usual to the middle. Zipping over, he gloved the ball, whirled, and made a throw that bounced a few feet to my right. As the runner's foot flew toward the base, I made the play. Keeping my left foot on the bag, I stretched my right leg and arm as far as I could, and snagged the ball in the webbing of my first baseman's glove!

Coach Spencer trotted out to congratulate me as well as Andy, a slender junior who stands an inch less than six feet and wears glasses. The coach patted Andy on the back and said something to him, and Scooter couldn't stop smiling as he hustled to the bench. Afterward, the coach grabbed my arm. "Way to go, James! You really showed your stuff at first base! Now when Lee bats in the seventh, I want you to show them your *pitching stuff*."

In the bottom of the sixth, we got a surprise, because it seemed like Butterfield found his energy reserve. He came out pitching as well as he did when the game opened. He struck out Dave Pankavich, Damon Vann, and Andy, mainly on curveballs. But his curve was dipping as well as breaking, so it looked like Butterfield had a new lease on life.

But at the end, you could tell Butterfield gave it his all for Lee. After he walked slowly to the bench, two or three guys hugged him. Flicking a smile, he took a seat, shook his head, and gulped water from a canteen.

In the top of the seventh, I went out to pitch for the first time on Jefferson's varsity. I'll admit that I felt nervous. With everyone in the crowd watching, I threw about ten warmups. Afterward, Herb trotted out for a talk.

Standing with his back to the bleachers, he pushed his iron-barred catcher's mask on top of his head and got right in my face. "James, my buddy, here's what you're gonna do. You're gonna give it your best shot and throw whatever pitch I call for. Trust me, you *can* get the ball over the plate. Now just *do it*, and *don't think* about it!"

Squeezing my left arm, he trotted back behind home plate and crouched, with his right knee on the ground. He held out his big mitt as an inviting target. Focusing, I thought, *Just do it*. I looked for the signs, and Herb's eyes seemed larger behind the mask. I wound up and threw two fastballs low, a curve which the right-handed batter took for strike one, and two more fastballs outside. I hated walking the first batter. That's a bad sign in baseball, but Coach Spencer and the guys in the field were yelling encouragement, and I tried to refocus.

The next batter was also right-handed, and I threw him a curve that he popped into short right field for a single. Now Lee had runners at first and second base. Up came the big guy, Bill McKinley. Again pitching from the stretch, I gave him a low curveball, and he shot a line drive into left center that turned into a double. The runner from second scored, and now they had runners at second and third with nobody out and hopes of expanding their 12-9 lead.

I stood there behind the board used for the pitcher's foot, dropping my gaze to the ground. Now hardly anyone in the stands was making noise.

"Snap out of it, James!" I looked up, and there stood Herb, Holding his mask and speaking in his strong voice. "So you're a little nervous, pal. You gotta get *over it.* You hear me?!"

He squeezed my left arm. "We're gonna win, and you're gonna save us." Nodding, he trotted back to home plate.

Facing Phil Moorbridge, Lee's other big hitter, I gave him two good curveballs, and he took both for strikes. Standing with my right foot on the pitcher's board and looking in for the sign, I watched the batter grinning at me. And I thought, *Does this guy think he's Casey at the Bat, taking two straight strikes?*

Herb signaled for my "drop ball," and suddenly I felt *ready*. A chill shot down my spine, and I shivered. Pitching from the stretch, I threw the ball and twisted my wrist just right, and from the follow-through, I watched the pitch spinning and bending, and he swung and missed, a split-second after the ball dropped below his knees!

"*Strike three!*" roared Mister Bronston, raising his right arm for the thumbs-up signal. After we heard a round of clapping and cheering from the Jefferson fans, Bronston motioned to the next batter. Taking his stance, their second baseman looked at me nervously like I was a star like Lefty Grove or Dizzy Dean.

Crouched behind the plate, Herb sees *everything*, and he's like a coach on the field. He called for curveballs, and the batter swung and missed two out of three. Next he signaled for the drop, and again I could feel the buzz. I took my stretch, checked the runners, and hurled a good drop that broke sharply down, and the batter just stood and watched it. "Strike three!" roared Bronston, again lifting his hand thumbs up!

Up came their big first baseman, Peter Rogers, a tough left-handed hitter who already blasted two doubles and a triple, but now he was facing a southpaw. When Herb signaled for an outside curve, I broke it outside, and Rogers swung and missed badly. *Strike one!*"

I smiled to myself, feeling like even Mister Bronston wanted me to succeed. Again Herb called for an outside curve, and this time the batter took it just off the plate. "*Strike two!*"

Rogers turned and glared at Bronston, but Herb stepped between them, pushed up his mask, and asked the umpire for another ball. Our history teacher-turned-umpire dug one out of his waist bag, and Herb tossed it to me. Gripping the ball and taking my stance, I saw the signal: fastball, but up *high*. Herb held his mitt chest high, and I knew we could fool Rogers. I wound up and threw my best fastball yet, and he watched it zip across the shoulders. "*Strike three! You're OUT!*"

Bronston waved his right hand thumbs up for the out, and people on our side of the bleachers exploded, clapping, cheering, and yelling! Above the others, I could hear Nat's voice: "*Way to go, brother!*" As I walked toward Jefferson's bench, I took a look at the bleachers. Seeing Linda and Iris and Nat and Wanda and many others cheering, I could have floated the rest of the way!

The bottom of the seventh unfolded like a baseball dream scripted by a famed sportswriter like Grantland Rice. First, their coach switched the second baseman, Paul O'Brien, according to Herb (who knows him), to pitcher, and Paul didn't have as much "stuff" on his pitches.

Bob James, a smart, fast, and good-hitting tenth grader who plays right field, led off with a first-pitch single. Taking a lead off first, Bob, a brown-haired fellow with brown eyes and strong arms, stared at the batter. When Dave Pankavich singled on the first pitch, Bob raced around to third.

Damon Vann, the shortstop, batted next. Damon, a medium-sized guy with brown eyes, curly brown hair, and an upbeat attitude, cracked the first pitch for a single to score the speedy James, and Pankavich, a senior who can run like the wind, reached third base easily. Scooter Thornton, another right-handed batter, singled to center. Andy's hit scored Pankavich, and the run cut Lee's lead to 12-11. Thornton looked at our bench from first base with a huge smile on his face!

Grinning, I turned and looked at the third base bleachers for the four girls and their reaction, but my eyes moved past them to a lanky-looking stranger with a fair complexion and sandy hair sitting at the end of the bleachers. For some reason he was staring at Nat. But the score was close, and I focused my attention on the game. Matt Richards, who had one single, came up next. Looking determined, he took a couple of practice swings and dug in at the plate.

O'Brien threw a sharp curve, and Matt popped it to the shortstop for the first out. He trotted back to the bench with his eyes on the ground, looking like he let the team down. Jack Jones stepped in next, swishing his bat back and forth like a tiger's tail. Taking his stretch, O'Brien threw a curveball above the knees, but Jack boomed a fly ball that carried to deep left center field, finally clearing the fence for a two-run home run! Thornton scored the tying run, and Jones, after trotting around the bases, jumped on home plate, giving Jefferson a 13-12 victory!

While we were congratulating Jack and each other, I stole another look into the stands. Not far beyond Nat I spotted the same guy I saw earlier. Taller than me, he was carefully making his way down the bleachers. Somehow he seemed familiar, but I didn't recognize him. He had sandy blond hair cropped short and a lanky frame, but he was older than high school age. Then it hit me: He could be a younger, slimmer Otto Herman.

But the excitement on the field drew my attention. Coach Spencer sent us over to congratulate the Lee players for giving their best effort. After that, we headed for the locker room. As I walked across the playground, Herb grabbed my arm. "I knew you'd get it *done*, James!"

He grinned. "You could use more game experience, but I love that *drop ball*, pal!"

III

At breakfast on Saturday, I was still feeling good about yesterday's last-inning victory. My mind kept going back over what happened in the game. I reflected on guys like Herb, Jack, Adam, Bob, Scott, Damon and Scooter all telling me my pitching "saved the day."

"James, are you *with us*?"

Sitting across the table from me, Natalia looked at me and grinned. I had a forkful of fried egg halfway to my mouth, and I must have been staring into space. I felt a blush in my cheeks, and I downed the eggs.

"Yes, James," Dad chimed in. "You may as well finish your breakfast." He had a twinkle in his eye, and Aunt Cora grinned too. I looked at the three of them, and our aunt made her usual comment: "You know, you don't want your food to get *cold*!"

Dad shifted gears smoothly. "Nat tells me you played well at first base in the win over Lee, and then you pitched the seventh inning. After giving up a walk and a hit, you struck out *three in a row*."

His smile encouraged me to talk about the game, and I gave Dad, Aunt Cora, and Nat a few highlights.

Afterward, Nat said brightly, "Dad, you must be *proud*. James is as important as anyone on Jefferson's team, and his friend Herb Jenkowski, the catcher. He's really a *star* too!"

When I started to reply, Nat switched topics. "By the way, James, I'm working on a paper for English, you know, the one about Thomas Jefferson's life after being President. I've searched through the pertinent books in the school library. Can you take me downtown today to the McIntire Public Library? Miss DeRoche said she understands they have quite a collection about Jefferson and his life. The library is on the corner of Second and Jefferson Streets."

"Sure, Sis. I can drop you off. I'll come back, handle the chores, and pick you up, whenever."

About an hour later Nat, carrying her cloth book bag for her notebooks and pencils, climbed in the pickup with me. We cruised along the driveway and turned toward town. On the way, she seemed her usual bubbly self, chatting about the game, the big hits, and my strikeouts.

We arrived at the McIntire Library with its brick walls, distinctive columns around the front door, and the balustrade around the top. After parking on Second Street, I watched Nat climb out. I looked at her through the open window. "It's about 10:15. When do you want me back?"

"Well, I really don't know. Why don't we say 1:00? If I find out that's too long, I'll call and leave a message with Aunt Cora. We can figure it out."

On that note I left, made a U-turn, and drove out of town, reaching home in fifteen minutes. Taking the hoe, I spent more than an hour hoeing and weeding our acre of garden. After that, I got out the lawn mower and cut the grass. When I finished, it was noon. By the time I returned to the kitchen and washed up, Aunt Cora had prepared a lunch of ham sandwiches, sliced apples, and coffee. Dad returned and washed up after plowing the back forty. When I sat at the table, he was sipping coffee and talking to Aunt Cora about what would be on the radio tonight.

After lunch, I brushed my teeth, changed clothes, and drove back to town. The clock on the dashboard said 12:45 when I parked on Jefferson Street, not far from the library. As I started to climb out of the truck, I spotted Nat on the corner talking to the tall sandy-haired young man I saw yesterday in the bleachers at our game. Surprised, I stopped and watched. I could see them smiling, nodding, and talking. In a few minutes he walked away.

I beeped the horn. Nat saw me, hurried over, and hopped in on the passenger's side. I started the engine and shifted gears. "Who's the guy I just saw you with?"

She looked at me with questioning eyes. "How *long* have you been parked here?"

Making the U-turn to drive out of town, I glanced at her. "I just parked a couple of minutes ago. I was about to get out when I saw you talking to the tall blond fellow. I didn't want to interrupt."

She smiled. "Well, you wouldn't have *interrupted* anything. I ran into him around 11:30 in the McIntire. He was looking for a book about Monticello, and a librarian helped him. At the circulation desk he saw me and introduced himself. His name is Ernie Herbert. He's the English fellow that Karl wrote to me about. Anyhow, Ernie and I began talking about what we're looking for, and he asked if I was hungry."

She grinned. "Well, I *was* hungry, and Ernie suggested we get lunch in the diner on University Avenue at The Corner. Well, we had a good lunch, and he seems like a really nice guy. He's manly and, well, rugged-looking. And he knows *a lot* about Monticello and Thomas Jefferson!"

By the time she finished, we were almost home. Sunshine made the day bright, a light breeze kept it cool, and the temperature felt like 70. We had our windows rolled down, and we didn't pass many cars on the road. Glancing at her, I remarked, "Does Ernie remind you of anyone?"

She studied me for several seconds. "What do you mean, 'remind me of anyone'?"

"He looks familiar to me, like someone we know, but who's older."

Nat gave me a blank stare. "Look, James. If you've got something to say, just tell me."

I wondered whether she thought he looked like Otto Herman, but I decided to skip it. Instead, I replied, "You know me, Sis. I'm always concerned about you."

As we turned in the driveway, I sensed her studying me. When I parked, she touched my arm. "Okay, Big Brother. I understand you caring about me. But really, I don't know much more about Ernie than he came to America from England this year. He wants to further his education, so he's thinking of enrolling at UVA. A couple of friends told him Virginia is a first-class university. He rents an apartment in town, and he drives a prewar black Buick. That's what I know."

Nat was on guard, so I didn't say any more about Ernie. Still, I had to wonder about a guy several years older who meets my attractive, bright, and outgoing sister, supposedly by coincidence. I decided to keep an eye on the new guy. To me it feels like something is wrong.

Chapter 5

School and Baseball

On Monday afternoon, when Nat and I came home from school, we sat at the kitchen table and chatted with Aunt Cora, who stopped cleaning to sit with us. Afterward, Nat and I each spent more than an hour doing homework in our rooms. It was a nice early summer day, except the wind was gusting 15 to 20 miles per hour. Still, that's good weather for working in a garden, and both of us did some hoeing and weeding.

Anyone who lives on a farm knows if you want to grow vegetables like tomatoes, green beans, peas, squash, and white potatoes, you need to plug away at hoeing and weeding almost daily. Further, we are often reminded that America is in the second full year of World War II, and we need to grow even more food than in 1942. Tough or not, more work must be done.

Again Nat asked me to look at changes she made in her paper about Jefferson's later life. Following dinner, I went up to my room, read it, and penciled in some minor revisions. Afterward, I went to her room and plopped the paper on her desk.

"What do you think, James? Did I make the improvements Miss DeRoche said I needed?"

I sat down on her bed. "Mostly you did, Sis. I'd say you will get at least a B."

Her countenance fell. "Why not an A?"

"It's hard to say, and Miss DeRoche might give you the A. I've had her for English, and I know she wants students to take a topic like yours, Jefferson at Monticello, and focus on a few highlights. But," and I tried to be diplomatic, "you can't include too much detail about too many different points of interest, because it weakens the main theme of your paper. And don't forget, she wants you to express yourself in *direct* sentences, that is, use the *active* voice, not the passive voice."

She looked at me like I was speaking Greek. "I don't get it."

"Okay, let's look at your first page." Picking up the paper, I read: "Jefferson was concerned with topics like science and natural history, so he was often immersed in reading books that he paid great sums of money for."

I eyed her. "The direct voice might say this: Jefferson concerned himself with educational matters such as science and natural history. In order to pursue those interests, he spent large sums of money purchasing important books to further his education."

"Wait a minute, James. What's the difference?"

"Look, Sis. I'm not a teacher, but I understand it like this. In the *active* voice, the subject *performs* the action of the verb. For example, 'The dog chased the cat.' In the passive voice, the subject *receives* the action of the verb. 'The cat was chased by the dog.'"

She looked at me and her eyes began sparkling as her smile expanded. "Okay … yeah, I think I get that."

Looking at me, she shook her head. "Why couldn't I see that *before*?"

I grinned. "Here's a rule of thumb I try to follow. Don't make your sentences too long. It's better to have two shorter sentences and make your points clearer, rather than to run two long sentences together. When you write longer sentences, you make it harder to avoid grammatical mistakes."

She was feeling better, and I added, "But remember this. Most of us make the same mistakes about using the correct grammar. So don't think you're the 'Lone Ranger' when it comes to learning better English."

She sighed. "I'll try and remember what you said, but if I need to, I can always ask, right?"

"Of course, Sis."

She smiled broadly. "Can I tell you something on a more personal level?"

Before I could reply, she continued: "I always keep my eyes and ears open. At the game on Friday, I couldn't help but hear Linda and Iris talking about boyfriends, partly because they were sitting right near Wanda and me. Well, those two are *really impressed* by you and Herb!"

Again Nat smiled. "One of these days I hope I can find a boyfriend who cares as much about me as Linda does about you and Iris does about Herb. But I'm saying that to you, and *nobody else*."

I stood up, and she jumped up and hugged me. "Also, I meant what I said after breakfast on Saturday. Dad is really *proud* of you! I know you hope to be as good a ballplayer as they say he used to be. Anyway, I'm *glad* to be your sister!"

I thanked her with a smile and headed to my room. I still had homework to do, but I wondered about calling Linda on a week night. Hearing an engine, I looked out and saw Dad parking the Chevy at the back of the driveway. I looked at the clock: 9:45. At first I wondered what he was doing, because he seldom leaves the house after a long day of work and a good dinner.

But I thought, *He went to see Helen LaSalle*. I wondered about that, but I dropped it because I figured Nat would uncover any interesting information. Once she did, she'd almost have to tell her brother. Smiling,

I sat at my desk and took out my Geometry assignment.

II

In the locker room after school on Tuesday, the players had finished pulling on their uniforms and tying the laces on their spikes by 3:30. Today we're playing at home against J.E.B. Stuart High, from Crozet, a growing town about 25 miles west of Charlottesville on Route 250. After I suited up, I noticed Coaches Spencer and Jackson conferring outside the cramped office they share beside the exit to the locker room. The equipment room occupies another small room next to theirs, and mainly Ray Riley uses it. Today Ray was already on the field, and he carried the bat bag with him.

The weather was looking overcast, and the sky threatened rain all afternoon. Most of us hoped the rain would hold off until following the game, but God decides that, not us. Coach Spencer posted today's lineup on the bulletin board between the two offices. By now everyone had checked the lineup at least once. Guys like Walt Bunker and Dave Pankavich are usually nervous about whether they're going to start, but both are good players, especially in the field. But everyone has "butterflies" on game day.

I figure it doesn't matter too much, because on a normal day we have 12 players in uniform. We started the season with 15 trying out, but one quit and two didn't make the cut. One sophomore, John Kilpatrick, has a parttime job at Mercy Hospital, so he gets excused from practice on certain days. I admire how Spencer always finds a way to use the non-starters, even if they play just one inning.

Today's lineup against Stuart High read like this:

Jack Jones, LF
Rob Henry, 2B
James Baker, 1B
Herb Jenkowski, C
Matt Richards, RF
Damon Vann, 3B
Dave Pankavich, CF
Walt Bunker, SS
Scott Matthews, P

"Okay, okay," declared Coach Spencer. *"Let's settle down!"*

When the coach took front and center, everyone waiting on the bench clammed up. "As you know, today we're playing J.E.B. Stuart High. Some of you are thinking they aren't very tough. But last Friday, that's what you thought about Lee High, *remember*?! Well, I made a couple of changes today, but if Stuart plays as well as they usually do, we're gonna need everyone on the team to do his best.

"In case you guys forget, Stuart competed for the state Class C championship last year. We're Class B, but we did *not* have a contending team. We had a very good team, but what I'm saying is because Stuart is smaller than Jefferson, that doesn't mean much in athletics."

Spencer cleared his throat. "Any questions?" He looked around, but no hands went up. "All right, then, let's hit the diamond!"

The coach waved for us to head outside. Everyone stood up, and we walked slowly across the concrete floor in our spikes. Once outside, it takes about 10 minutes and we're on the ball field playing catch. At the same time, Stuart kept going with batting practice.

Today I played catch with Herb and Bob James, who started in right field last week. Bob is our backup catcher, and he can play the outfield and pitch, too. He stood beside me, and Herb alternated his throws between us. After a few minutes, Herb started blazing throws to Bob. Since both play catcher, they need to practice on catching fast balls.

Glancing around, Herb said, "I've got a couple of friends in Crozet. One's my cousin Steve Majeski. Steve tells me their big guns this year are a tall pitcher, Oscar Smithson, and he's got plenty of stuff. They also have a real good center fielder, Joe Greenburg, and a third baseman, Mickey Kellner. All three of those guys can really swing that bat and throw that ball!"

Coach Spencer waved for us to begin batting practice, since Stuart had finished theirs. Spencer walked out to the pitcher's rubber and loosened up. The coach throws each of us one fastball and one curve, and he repeats it for maybe six swings. Usually he throws every pitch over the plate, but in a different location. Spencer is forever telling us that we need to hit a pitch no matter the location, low, outside, inside, or high, as long as you think the ball is a strike.

A couple of years ago I read a newspaper story about Ted Williams, the Red Sox star since 1939, and now he's in the Air Force. The sportswriter said Williams won't swing at a pitch out of the strike zone. They say Ted is well known for telling hitters to be selective with the strikes you hit. Make sure the ball is in your "Happy Zone," which means your favorite hitting area. Ted Williams' ideas sound good to me, and he batted .406 in 1941. I mean, *nobody* bats .400!

The game started, and soon it turned into a pitching battle between Scott Matthews and Oscar Smithson, Stuart's right-hander. Smithson can fire fastballs like a machine. What saved us is that his control of pitches was erratic, and he walked nine. Matthews, a right-hander who throws pretty good fastballs, has a real bender for his curve. Scott had their hitters getting set for the fastball, but whenever he gets two strikes on the batter, Scott breaks his curveball over the outside corner.

We were really yelling when he fanned hard-hitting Joe Greenburg *twice*. The second time Scott nailed Greenburg on a low curve, and he flung his bat over his bench into foul territory by the screen! That display got him a warning from Mister Bronston, and it gave all of us a smile.

When we reached the seventh, the score was tied, 1-1. Both teams scored once in the sixth, mainly due to the pitchers getting tired. I know fastballs can wear a batter down, but after a while, they wear down the pitcher, too. Stuart scored their run on two walks and a single. We scored our run on walks to Jack Jones and Rob Henry, and my single to left center. We almost scored a second run on Herb's bouncer over the pitcher's head, but their shortstop made the grab in front of second base, whipped a dart to home plate, and the catcher tagged out Rob, who was sliding, after he missed Coach Jackson's signal to hold up at third base.

In the seventh with two outs, Stuart scored when the third batter walked, and the next guy grounded to shortstop, but Walt Bunker muffed it, and both runners were safe. Up came Mickey Kellner, their hard-hitting third baseman, who hit hard line drives in his first three at-bats, but all three were caught. Coach Spencer went out and talked to Scott, I think mainly to give him a break. Anyway, Kellner belted a curveball to the bottom of the right field fence, and that blast that scored one run. Matthews recorded the third out by fanning the next batter on a sharp curve, but we trailed, 2-1.

A close game seems to encourage people to buy more refreshments. It turns out the refreshments nearly sold out. Mister Knudson, our bright, witty, and well-read Social Studies teacher who can crack a joke, was working in the booth along with Miss Martin, the dark-haired, brown-eyed librarian who teaches Mathematics.

During the game, most of us noticed the steady stream of folks coming from the refreshment booth behind the bleachers, all carrying bags of popcorn, candy bars, or soft drinks. The next day at school, I heard that Miss Martin kept telling her students not only did Jefferson set a school record for refreshment sales, but the soda pop actually ran out in the fifth inning! Herb told us he saw her smiling like a movie star who received an Academy Award!

Returning to the seventh inning: Smithson struck out the first batter, Dave Pankavich. With one out, Walt, after missing two fastballs, poked a single over second base. Up came Scott, and he blasted a fastball for a double that rattled off the chain link fence in left center, but Coach Jackson held up Walt at third.

That brought Jack Jones up to the plate, and I'm thinking *If Jack doesn't get a hit, we're down to Rob, and he already struck out three times.* I glanced down the bench, and the expressions I saw showed other guys had the same thought.

Smithson fooled Jack twice, the first time with a high fastball and the second time with a sharp-breaking curve. Kids in the stands were pleading for Jack to get a hit. Even Coach Spencer yelled "You can hit this guy, Jack! Show him you're the *big hitter*!"

Smithson took his time in the stretch, glaring at Jack for several seconds. Finally he threw the hardest curveball we saw all afternoon, but Jack connected with a mighty swing that rocketed the ball on a low line into deep center, and the ball cleared the center fielder's head and clanked into the fence on the fly! Walt trotted in from third base, Scott zipped around from second, and we won, 3-2!

The crowd exploded with cheering and clapping! People of all ages, even a couple of grandfathers, came running onto the field, but Coach Spencer reached Jack first! Everyone was slapping Jack on the back, shaking hands, and congratulating each other! What a scene! I saw Herb hugging Jack near home plate, and I swear I saw tears in those guys' eyes. I can tell you that was an afternoon and a ball game to remember!

At dinner Nat couldn't tell Dad and Aunt Cora enough about what a wonderful game our school played. She even made a highlight out of my single off their star pitcher. Dad and Cora asked me about the game, and I focused on Scott's good pitching, Herb's fine catching, and Jack's booming double to center that drove home the tying and winning runs. I'm not big on blowing my own horn, so I feel good just basking in the glory of my teammates.

Later, just before bedtime, I heard Nat chatting with a couple of friends on the phone. After she finished, I went upstairs to my bedroom and pulled on my pajamas. All the while I was mulling over the personal information that Herb confided to me earlier, after we showered and dressed and went out to climb into our cars to drive home.

In the school parking lot following the game, Herb came up to me. After glancing around, he spoke in a lower tone than usual. "There's something I need to tell you about your father."

When I nodded, he continued: "Diagonally across the street from Jack's Grocery is a nice restaurant, Harry's Fine Food. I've been thinkin' about this, because I just happened to see it last night. I was gettin' into our Dodge, which I parked on the street close to Jack's. On the other side, I noticed a familiar Chevrolet, and I realized it's your father's car, the car you drove when we took the girls to see *Casablanca*. Anyway, your dad and this good-looking, dark-haired woman walked out of Harry's, and he helped her get in the car. After he got in behind the wheel, they sat there and talked."

Herb took a deep breath. "Well, James, maybe I shouldn't have, but I just kept watching. Your dad must like the woman, because he kissed her more than once before he started the engine." He paused. "I hate to tell you this, but if it was *my dad*, well, I'd want to know."

We looked at each other for a few moments. "Actually, Herb, I know who you mean, because we go to the same church. Her name is Helen LaSalle. You and I are good friends, and I'm glad you told me. But how about if we keep this secret, you know, between us?"

He flicked a smile. "Agreed, pal!" He reached over and squeezed my upper arm, like he does when he's with a friend. "Hang in there, and I'll see you tomorrow at school."

On that note, Herb climbed into the family car and headed for home, and I drove home too. I fell asleep that night thinking about what Herb said and wondering if I should tell my sister.

III

The rest of the week went rather well, both at school and at home with homework and chores. I decided to think a little more about Dad and

Missus LaSalle before revealing my secret to Nat. For one thing, she's likely to talk about it to friends, and I don't want Herb's name involved. He's a good friend, but he's like a clam when it comes to stuff you tell him in confidence. And that's the way it ought to be.

We won game number three on Friday afternoon against Culpepper High, in Culpepper, which is about an hour's school bus ride north of Charlottesville. The nice thing about away games is we get excused early from our 2:00 classes, but that's after having teachers sign our permission cards and give us homework assignments. We made the long ride by traveling north on US-29.

Coach Spencer is pleased with how we won on Tuesday against Jeb Stuart High, and he made only a couple of changes in the lineup. He started Rob Henry at pitcher, and Rob is a sophomore who pitched last year in the summer league. But today would be Rob's first varsity game. A quiet guy, he's got red hair, green eyes, pale skin, and a slender frame, and Nat likes him. A right-hander, Rob throws mostly curveballs, but he has a kind of sneaky fastball. Bob James took over in right field, and Andy Thornton played second base.

Culpepper High is rated Class C, so we play them just once a year. On the bus Herb was telling us Culpepper won about half their games in 1942, so maybe they won't be too tough this year. But Coach Spencer gave his usual pregame pep talk, telling us that some of our players might think the other school isn't as good as we are, but we need to go all-out in every game.

It turned out Herb was on target. We romped all over Culpepper, 11-3. Rob pitched well for the first five innings, and Walt pitched the last two. I had a single and a double. Herb hit four straight singles, two of them driving in runs. Jack unloaded a home run and a triple, and only two great catches by their center fielder prevented a higher score. Bob cracked two singles, and he was all smiles. Scott Matthews hit a pair of doubles, so he was back on track. Even Rob, not always dependable at the plate, contributed by walking three times and hitting a single in the seventh.

We had fun on the bus ride home. Coach Spencer always sits in the front seat behind Ray Riley, the driver, and Coach Jackson occupies the other front seat behind the steps and the door. For a pleasant surprise, Coach Spencer told Ray to stop at a crossroads diner, and the coach bought everyone a hamburger and a Coca-Cola. The rest of the way we ate hamburgers, drank Cokes, and laughed and talked about the game. When I walked in the back door, it was 6:45.

I felt tired as well as exhilarated. If you ever played on a JV or varsity school team, you have experienced the special kind of feeling that comes from winning a game. I suppose it's partly why so many young people like playing sports. I know it's a powerful feeling that's hard to match anywhere else.

After dinner, I sat at the table and talked with Dad and Aunt Cora. They seemed keen on hearing details of the game, and I felt good about giving them the highlights. Tonight Nat listened closer, I think because the game wasn't at home, so she couldn't attend. All the while I sensed a little uneasiness between our father and our aunt, and I could tell Nat noticed it too. The atmosphere just felt different, maybe because of what Herb told me about Dad and Missus LaSalle.

While Dad and Aunt Cora lingered at the table drinking coffee and making conversation, I volunteered to help Nat clean up the kitchen. After washing the dishes, Nat said she needed to call Wanda. She dialed the number on the wall phone, and I could hear her talking as I wiped the dishes and put them away.

After hanging up, Nat came over and asked, "James, tomorrow morning I need to do more research at the city library. Can you take me and pick me up again?"

"Sure, I'll be glad to. In fact, I may go and look for a baseball bat at Jameson's Book Store at The Corner. They sell a lot of sports equipment."

When I spoke, Dad gave me an inquiring look. I said, "Well, I cracked my bat in the game, but I didn't notice it until I got home. I'd rather buy a new one than use one of the school's old bats. Only a couple of those bats are new this season."

Dad smiled. "No problem, son. You sure can't hit as well with that cracked bat."

Curious, I asked what he did when his bat cracked. "A fair question," Dad replied. "Mostly I used bats made of northern ash, and of course, that's if the local sporting goods store carried them. Ash is a *dense* wood. Anyway, I always thought ash bats felt better when you swing and connect, you know, when you *really* hit a pitch."

Lying on my bed later that evening, I read more of my current novel, Agatha Christie's *The Body in the Library*. I'm really impressed with Miss Christie's ability to create a twisted plot, intriguing characters, and oddball situations. Of course, I also love her clever writing style because she keeps you guessing until the end about who committed the murder, and how, and especially *why*.

By the time I set the book on the nightstand, my eyes were feeling grainy, and I was having a hard time focusing on the story. Drifting off into dreamland, I visualized myself batting in the seventh inning of a big game on a sunny afternoon. After swinging and seeing two curveballs dip around my bat, I looked out and saw the huge green-eyed pitcher with stubble on his chin looking at me. Winding up, he fired a blazing fastball. Ready and waiting, I timed it correctly, swung smoothly, and slugged a long fly ball to left field.

Looking out toward left as I ran around first base, I saw the baseball sprout tiny wings, and the flapping wings lifted it toward a huge cloud with two blue eyes. Suddenly an eagle with long brown wings swooped down, grabbed the bill in its beak, and rose majestically until the bird and the ball vanished between the cloud's eyes, one of which slowly winked at me.

Chapter 6

Bats and Secrets

Opening my eyes on Saturday morning, I sat up and looked out the window at a bright sunny day. My black alarm clock said 6:20. Slowly I got up, pulled on my jeans and a tee shirt, and went to our upstairs bathroom to shave and clean up. Ten minutes later, sitting on my bed, I thought about today's events. Sometime this morning I needed to take Nat to the city library, and Dad said I could use the Chevrolet. I thought more about Walt and Wanda, and I decided to call him later. Maybe we could plan a double date to the movies.

After breakfast, I went outside and weeded the garden for a while. When Nat yelled my name, I stood up and looked at her. She was standing on the back porch waving at me. When I reached the porch, she asked if I was ready to leave. I freshened up at the kitchen sink, picked up the Chevy keys, and in no time we were driving toward town. I dropped her off, decided to postpone looking for a new bat, and drove home to do more chores.

When I parked near the end of the driveway, I saw Dad coming in from the barn. I hopped out of the car, and he asked, "Would you like to see my baseball equipment?"

I said yes, and we headed for the back door. On the porch he observed, "I see you delivered your sister to the library."

Nodding, I followed him inside. Aunt Cora was mopping the kitchen floor, and she stopped, looked at us, and wiped her forehead with a white handkerchief. She eyed Dad. "So what are you men up to?"

He grinned, "James and I are going to look at baseball bats. Are you interested too?"

She grinned as if he had cracked a joke. "No, thank you, Zeke. I'll stick to my kitchen tasks."

She returned to mopping while we walked into the good-sized room off the dining room that Dad uses for a den. The room has pastel blue walls, a white ceiling, and classy furniture, including two blue mohair easy chairs, two walnut hand-crafted bookcases filled with books, a mahogany writing desk with a blue upholstered chair, and a large oak curio cabinet with glass in the doors.

Dad unlocked and opened the glass doors. Slowly he removed three weathered bats, one by one. He handled them carefully like they were part of the family fortune. I could see the faraway look that came into his eyes when he picked up a dark wooden bat.

Gripping the bat, he stepped back, took a right-handed batting stance, looked at an imaginary pitcher, and swung the bat once, slowly. "This may suit your purpose," he said, with a twinkle in his eyes. "Lou Gehrig mostly used this kind of ash bat. I've read that Babe Ruth swung bats as long as 38 to 40 inches, and they weighed 40 or more ounces. Gehrig, they say, used shorter bats, about 34 or 35 inches long."

He smiled at me. "Those were *big bats*, son. I don't care who says otherwise."

He turned the dark bat over in his suntanned hands. "Babe Ruth's bats were what I call *war clubs*. Most of my friends couldn't get around with those bats! No matter. I acquired this Lou Gehrig model in Washington, DC, in early 1929, and I only used it in a handful of games."

He handed me the bat, and I gripped it. Looking at the bat, I swished it back and forth a couple of times. I was awestruck. When I started to speak, no words came.

"You don't need to thank me. One day I want you to pass on your baseball equipment to your kids." He studied my eyes as tears blurred my vision. We embraced for an eternal second, and he stepped back. "Why don't we go out in the side yard and you hit me a few fly balls?"

Without waiting for the answer, he dug into the bottom of the cabinet. As I stood and watched, he pulled out a worn five-finger Rawlings Glove with very little webbing between the thumb and first finger. He also retrieved two scuffed baseballs. He headed for the back door, and I followed with the bat, grabbing my ball glove on the way. Aunt Cora smiled as we walked through the kitchen, and all I could think was, *Boy, this is going to be fun.*

In the yard we moved a good distance apart. Like the coach does in practice, I tossed up a ball and hit a high fly that carried maybe 200 feet. Each time I knocked a high fly, Dad floated effortlessly under the descending ball, and snagged it in the glove he had used for years.

Oddly enough, I seemed to be living a dream where everything I've learned about baseball from my father came back in person. After ten minutes, we switched places. Dad took the bat, tossed the ball up with one hand, and with both hands demonstrated his smooth swing. He belted an endless stream of high fly balls that made me run left and right and back and forth just in time to catch all but a couple of them. After nearly an hour, we had enjoyed quite a workout!

Dad raised an arm and declared, "Let's hang it up for today, James!"

Taking our equipment, we returned to the kitchen, where Aunt Cora was sitting at the table. After placing the bat, balls, and gloves in one corner. Reaching into the fridge, Dad took out a jug of lemonade, filled two tall glasses, and handed me one. Smiling, Aunt Cora followed us with her eyes as we walked through the house and out on the front porch. There we relaxed in two of the wooden chairs and sipped lemonade.

While we took it easy, Dad told me a few baseball stories. One of my favorites was about a game he had played in the local summer league around 1930. He struck out three times against a red-headed, broad-shouldered right-hander who threw a "sneaky curve" with a delivery that made it look like a fastball. In the bottom of the seventh with his team down 4-3 and a runner at second, Dad took a wide-breaking curve for strike one.

On the second pitch, he said, looking at me, "I just knew that big redhead was gonna throw that tricky curve. He did, but this time I was ready, and *boy*! When I took my swing, everyone at that little ballpark could hear the *crack* of the bat." Stopping he sipped lemonade. "And for me, I can still see that white ball flying well beyond the fence in left field!"

Dad smiled. Glancing over at me, he nodded. "Well, James, that's enough of the good old days! I've got some things to get done. Let's go inside."

We got up, and I followed Dad into the kitchen. Putting our glasses in the sink, Dad picked up his equipment and went into the den. I picked up my ball glove and the ball and went upstairs to my bedroom. Sitting n the bed, I knew that magical time with my father is etched forever in my memory. I was bursting with pride.

II

After lunch with Dad and Aunt Cora, I drove the Chevy into town to pick up Nat. When I approached the McIntire Library, I saw her standing out in front and chatting with Ernie Herbert. As I parked at the curb, she pointed in my direction, and he followed her to the car.

Climbing out of the sedan, I approached them with a smile. "James," she said, "this is Ernie Herbert. He came to Charlottesville from New York, and before that, from England. He's working part-time and thinking about attending the University of Virginia."

A lanky fellow maybe an inch taller than me, Ernie looked me over like I was a scientific specimen. He has sandy blonde hair, wide blue eyes, broad shoulders, and he has a faint air of superiority. He stood erectly as if he had been called to attention. I thought, *He might say he's from England, but he acts more like a German.*

As I evaluated him, Nat introduced me. "Ernie, this is my older brother James. He does real well in school, he helps dad run the farm, and he's quite the baseball player!"

"Yes, James. How are you?" Grinning, Ernie vigorously pumped my hand using a grip of iron. "I am working at Jameson's Book Store, and I often go to the McIntire to read up on American topics. Life seems so different here, and more tranquil. The war is crushing England, and I hate the war. That's why I left. Luckily, I found passage on a ship to New York."

Knowing what Karl wrote to Nat about Ernie, I shifted gears. "You're thinking of enrolling at the University of Virginia? I'm surprised UVA would have the academic reputation to attract students from as far away as England."

He looked curiously at me. "Well, no. I learned of the university from Karl Ellis. Before I arrived in New York, I hadn't heard of your university. I guess that's because my friends are mostly English."

I nodded. "But you are correct. Virginia, or UVA as people around here call it, is a highly rated academic institution. I hope to attend myself after I graduate next June."

Nat, who was listening, smiled, but she looked at me with pleading eyes. "Ernie has invited me to visit his apartment at The Corner, and I'm hoping you'll come too."

I smiled. "Sure, Nat, I'm happy to go." Turning to him, I added, "I'll drive, and that way you won't need to bring us back here."

"Yes, *sir*! That sounds very good!" Ernie smiled at Nat. "Why don't you two follow me?"

Wheeling around, he walked rapidly toward a black Buick parked on the far side of the library. Watching him, I thought he seemed to strut. When he said "good," I notice it sounded like *goodt*. Turning away, I walked with Nat to the Chevy.

As I opened the door, I saw Ernie pointing in the direction of The Corner. Starting the engine, I followed the Buick. Ten minutes later I parked across the street from the Chancellor's Building at The Corner. We climbed out, followed Ernie around the side of the building, and came to a heavy brown door.

Ernie entered, Nat followed, and I came last. In the small foyer we passed a bank of mailboxes, and we climbed an old wooden staircase. Upstairs, we followed Ernie along a dimly lit hallway with worn brown carpet. The smell of yesterday surrounded us like an unseen cloud. At the next to last apartment, he stopped. Retrieving keys from his pocket, he unlocked the door.

Motioning us inside first, he followed and closed the door. The low-ceiling main room had a carpet of faded blue floral designs. For furniture the room had a dull orange couch along the left wall, two oak captain's chairs on the opposite side, and a small table with two chairs in a kitchenette with a humming white refrigerator. The door to another room was next to the fridge. Beside the second door hung two prints of England, one of the London Bridge and the other of a sloping field dotted by gray sheep. I watched Nat take it all in with her inquiring eyes.

Ernie grabbed her hand. "Come, Natalia. Let me show you my writing desk and the materials in the bedroom."

Appearing hesitant, she nevertheless agreed. "Sure, I like to write too."

Ernie opened the door, and the three of us went into the bedroom. The single bed was neatly made. We moved over to a worn pine rolltop desk with drawers on the right. Half a dozen books were stacked against the right support. In the middle I saw a writing pad, several pencils, a fountain pen, and a pot of blue ink, all lined up neatly.

He beamed. "I'm writing my impressions of what life in your country is like. Already I have one chapter written!"

Nat smiled. "This seems pretty nice."

Ernie nodded vigorously. "Yes, this apartment is close enough to the university that I can continue my part-time job, walk to classes, buy what I need at The Corner, and live comfortably."

He walked out of the bedroom and toward the kitchenette, and Nat followed. He seemed to want to extol the apartment's features, but I'd seen and heard enough. Staying behind, I looked over the books. One caught my eye: *Jefferson's Albemarle*, compiled by the WPA. Picking it up, I flipped several pages.

The next one I picked up was *The Living Jefferson*, by James Truslow Adams. I knew Nat was reading up on Jefferson and Monticello, and I recall Mister Bronston mentioning this book as a good source. In the tenth grade I once checked it out from the school library when I was writing a term paper on Jefferson. I turned a few pages, and a photo fell out.

I picked it up. The sepia-toned picture showed a young man with light hair about my height who didn't look much older than me. He stood proudly on a street corner with several venerable buildings behind him, notably a cathedral. When I studied the photo, I realized the man looked like a young Otto Herman. Turning it over, I saw one word printed on the back: Marienplatz.

At that moment I heard Nat calling from the kitchenette. I put the picture back in the book, returned the book to its place, and joined them. "What have you been doing, Big Brother?"

"Oh, just looking at Ernie's books." I turned to him. ""I see you have one from the McIntire called *The Living Jefferson*. That book should have plenty about Thomas Jefferson and Monticello."

"Yes, well," Ernie replied. "I'm quite interested in Thomas Jefferson, because he was an early American President who had a great interest in freedom and liberty, including to free slaves. Recently, I read that Jefferson freed all of his slaves when he died in 1826."

I was quite sure that because of debts, Jefferson had freed just a few slaves upon his death, but Nat interrupted my thoughts. "Well, James, we must go. I have to work on my paper this afternoon."

Turning to Ernie, she smiled. "It's nice of you to show us your apartment. One of these days I hope to have a place in town and attend the University of Virginia myself." Her eyes sparkled. "Yes, Ernie, your apartment is really *quite nice*."

"Of course," he replied, looking around. "However, do not be too surprised if I'm living somewhere else soon. I took this furnished apartment right away when I arrived, before I had time to look around. I haven't signed the lease yet, and this place is rather expensive. On the other hand, if all goes well, I might decide to keep it."

Ernie walked out with us, and once outside, Nat smiled and thanked him again. He stood and watched us walk to the car. I started the engine, and we drove away on University Avenue. All the way home Nat chattered about Ernie, pronouncing him "a real nice guy with a nice apartment."

But I had my suspicions, beyond his false comment about Jefferson's slaves. The picture hidden in the book that I accidentally found seemed to connect Ernie Herbert with the deceased Otto Herman. I wondered if the two were related. But if so, why did Ernie come to Charlottesville? Is he what he appears to be, or not? I needed to think it over.

III

On Sunday, May 2, Dad, Aunt Cora, Nat, and I attended church, but after the worship service, Dad surprised us. The four of us were greeted by Reverend Benjamin just outside the doors, and we started toward our Chevrolet. As we did, Dad took Aunt Cora's hand. "Do you mind if I invite Helen LaSalle and her girl Joyce over to our house for lunch?"

The incredulous look I saw in Aunt Cora's eyes virtually defied description, and Nat's mouth sagged open. Caught off guard, I had to catch my breath.

But Aunt Cora rose smoothly to the occasion. "No, Zeke. I don't mind *at all*. But what we have t eat is the makings of sandwiches, plenty of iced tea, and chocolate chip cookies that I baked yesterday. Do you think that will be *enough* for guests?"

Assuring her the fare would be fine, Dad turned and walked over to greet Missus LaSalle, who stood on the edge of the church plaza holding Joyce's hand. I knew Dad had taken her to dinner, and Nat and I watched him. He said something to her, and she blushed. But in a few moments she nodded. When she did, Dad brought her and her girl over to where we waited.

"Helen," Dad said, "I'd like to introduce you to my family. This is Cora, my sister-in-law who lives with us." The two women shook hands politely, and Aunt Cora offered her sweet smile.

Dad turned to us. "This is my son James, and my daughter Natalia, whom we usually call *Nat*." My sister and I smiled, and we also shook hands. Missus LaSalle looked us over, and she smiled.

Dad looked pleased. "And this little person is Joyce, Helen's daughter." After we greeted her, he added, "As I believe you know, Helen is our church secretary."

Motioning at our car, Dad added, "We can all ride in our Chevrolet, Helen. Afterward, I can bring you and Joyce back to your car."

At first Missus LaSalle looked a bit uncomfortable, but soon she agreed. "Yes, Zeke. I'm sure my car will be all right parked in the church lot."

We walked to the Chevrolet. Dad held the front door for Missus LaSalle, and she slipped gracefully into the seat. Aunt Cora, holding Joyce on her lap, sat in back with Nat and I. Dad started the engine, and he drove slower than usual to our house. During the drive, he chatted with Helen, and Aunt Cora entertained Joyce, starting with, "Do you like school, sweetie?"

Joyce looked at the three of us, one by one, and from the front her mother said, "Go ahead and tell them, Joyce." Turning toward us, Missus LaSalle added, "Yes, she likes kindergarten. She can write *all* of her letters. And, she can read the *Dick and Jane* which the first graders use."

By the time Dad parked in the driveway, Joyce, evidently at ease, was regaling us with what she knew about Dick, Jane, and Spot along with what fun she has at school. As we walked into the kitchen, Aunt Cora looked at Dad. "I'll make lunch, Zeke, Why don't you and Helen sit on the front porch and relax." Again she smiled. "Maybe Nat can help me."

Aunt Cora leaned forward toward Joyce. "Sweetheart, would you like to help us?"

Joyce looked up at her mother, who nodded, and the child replied, in a small voice, "Yes, I would like to help."

Watching, Nat smiled at her. "Yes, Joyce, helping Aunt Cora will be fun, won't it?"

The little girl's head nodded like a bobber with a fish, and Nat turned to me. "James, you can join Dad and Missus LaSalle on the front porch, can't you?"

Having no plans, I agreed. Smiling to myself, I followed them through the house and out on the porch, where each of us sat in a wooden chair. Dad and Missus LaSalle sat next to each other, and I moved my chair beside hers. The situation felt awkward, but I knew it would last just a few minutes.

Missus LaSalle started with an innocuous question: "Zeke, did you grow up in this area?"

Dad nodded, looking at the distant landscape. "Yes, I was born and raised in Charlottesville, and I've spent much of my life working the land on this farm."

He turned to face her. "These days I get great help from James, and, who knows? Maybe one day he'll operate this farm on his own, or with his family."

Taking a look at me, she smiled, her blue eyes dancing. Turning to Dad, Missus LaSalle said, "You've told me about your wife Mary being killed in the traffic accident a few years ago, so I guess your sister-in-law came to live with you some time after that."

Dad glanced at her, and he looked up at the cloudless blue sky like the answer was hidden there.

"Well, I usually don't say much about my wife's death, although it's no secret. But now that you ask, Cora endured the death of her husband, Joe Raleigh. Uncle Joe, as we called him, died of pneumonia in February of 1936. They lived in Richmond at the time. Mary, as I mentioned before, died when she was hit by a drunk driver in the middle of 1937. Cora came to live with us a couple of months later. Not only is she a huge help around here, but she's almost a second mother to James and Natalia."

Naturally I was listening, and I'm always pleased to hear Dad talk about our mother, even though I've heard it before. In a few moments, he turned to Missus LaSalle. "You moved here from Roanoke a few months back, if I understand what you said the other night. If you don't mind the question, did your husband die, or what?"

She looked at him calmly. "Well, he died, but like you, I don't talk much about painful personal things. Of course, it's hard on my sweet Joyce, so I'm careful about what I say in front of her."

Smiling quickly, she looked off in the distance herself. But just then Nat appeared at the screen door. "Aunt Cora says lunch is ready!"

Nat held the screen door open, and we moved inside, with Missus LaSalle going first and Dad following her. In the kitchen, Aunt Cora indicated the two of them should sit on one side of the table, and Nat and I on the other side. "I'll sit at the end, and Joyce can sit on the end near her mother. If anybody needs something, I can get it."

I remembered Aunt Cora felt uneasy around Dad's lady friend when we met at the restaurant, so I wondered if she was being extra polite. I took a chair beside my sister, Joyce climbed into the open chair, and Dad said grace.

Aunt Cora passed around a plate of ham and cheese sandwiches along with a peanut butter and jelly sandwich for Joyce. Everyone's glass had been filled with iced tea, including a smaller glass for Joyce. A large plate filled with Ritz Crackers and chocolate chip cookies crowned the center of the table.

Twenty minutes later, after we finished eating, Missus LaSalle stood up and announced she had housework to do, so she and Joyce needed to leave. "Zeke, if you would be kind enough to drive us back to the church, I would appreciate it."

Smiling, she moved over to Aunt Cora, thanked her, and shook her hand daintily. The apparent rivals for Dad's affections smiled politely at each other. By that time I had figured what Helen LaSalle said and did in front of us, she was doing mainly for show. Trying to be discreet, Nat was watching everyone like a hawk. I could almost see her mental wheels turning, and I stifled a smile.

After we said goodbyes all around, Dad left to drive Missus LaSalle and Joyce back to the church. As soon as they walked out the door, Nat started helping Aunt Cora clean up the kitchen. Rather than watch my sister with our aunt, I went upstairs to the sanctuary of my room.

Lying on my bed, I rested for a while. In my mind I turned over the events of the morning, the ride home, the conversation on the porch, and the lunch. First, I had to admit being surprised that Dad made the invitation. He seemed to be sending a message to all of us, but especially to Aunt Cora. But if so, he handled it as smooth as silk. To use a baseball analogy, Aunt Cora belted a slow curveball for an extra base hit. Thinking about her just made me smile.

On the other hand, I had to admit that Missus LaSalle handled her end of the event every bit as smoothly. She spoke casually with Dad on the porch without revealing much about herself. She handled the conversation nicely at lunch, but *nobody* said anything really important. Still, I figured Helen LaSalle came across more like an actress than a widow.

Interrupting my thoughts, Nat burst into the room, closed the door, and plopped down in the desk chair. She stared at me for several long seconds. Finally, she nodded. "Listen, James, and let me tell you what I think. I don't know *whether* Aunt Cora or Missus LaSalle gave the better performance, but I felt like nobody said anything to reveal his or her *true feelings*."

She grinned wickedly. "Don't tell me, Big Brother, that you didn't catch onto *that*!"

Again I had to smile. "Actually, I caught most of it, but I figured you'd see more than me." Nat started to reply, but I held up a hand. "I will say that Dad does seem *sweeter* on Helen LaSalle than either of us thought. There for a while I thought he was moving toward a romantic relationship with Aunt Cora, because he kept dropping hints. But after today, I'd say no dice."

"Well, James, if this situation continues, we could be looking at a stepmother in the not-too-distant future. But I can promise you this. Something just feels *wrong*."

I raised my eyebrows, and she continued: "While you were out front, I sat with Joyce at the kitchen table. She's a nice little girl, and she seems to like me, so I offered to teach her to print her name. When I said that, she told me she *knows* how to print her name. I smiled, got a pencil and paper, and handed them to her. She took the pencil and printed J-A-N-E-T. When I said she spelled *Janet*, not *Joyce*, she looked at me with fear in her eyes."

"Of course, I tried to reassure her." Frowning, Nat rolled her eyes. "I said nicely, 'Don't worry about it.' Well, Joyce flashed her little smile, and quite innocently she said, 'See, when we were in Roanoke, my name was Janet.' At that point I figured something is wrong, so I dropped the name stuff. I asked if she wanted to help me set the table, and she did, so we did it together."

Nat gave me a slow smile. "I'd say what Joyce let out about her name tells me that her mother simply is *not* telling us the truth about their life in Roanoke."

As I considered what she said, Nat leaned forward. "I hope you noticed that if Missus LaSalle is present, Joyce looks to her before answering any question. It's like the mother has turned the child into a puppet, and she uses her to conceal their real background."

Before I could agree, Nat stood up. "I'm sorry, James, but you *need* to know this stuff. So what's *really* going on with this Missus LaSalle and her daughter?"

"I don't know, Nat, but yes, I noticed what you saw. I agree about Joyce. She told you something she wouldn't have said with her mother present. By the way, I thought Helen and Aunt Cora both put on a show for Dad's benefit, *and* for ours. My conclusion is that we need to know more about what's up with the LaSalle's."

We embraced, Nat smiled at me, and she left, closing the door. Standing there considering my sister's observations, I knew we needed to investigate Helen LaSalle's background.

Chapter 7

Digging for the Truth

The idea of checking up on Helen LaSalle nagged at me all day Monday, but I made it through my classes in good shape. After school we had the usual day-before-game workout, including plenty of batting practice. Everyone knows that tomorrow we have a home game against Waynesboro High. In the locker room after practice, Coach Spencer sat us on the side bench.

"Okay fellas, listen up!" He glared at Jack Jones who was whispering to someone, and Jack fell silent. "Okay, then," and the coach ran his gaze over us. "So far you know we're pretty good. We're 3-0, and who knows? Maybe we can win a few more!"

He grinned, with his eyes bright. "We had a good practice today, and we should be ready. The lineup for Waynesboro will be posted before 3:00 tomorrow. If any of you are hurt, or whatever, let me know. Walt has a sore arm, but nothing too bad. Coach Jackson and I have some things we can do for aches and pains." Spencer glanced at Coach Jackson, and he nodded.

"All right, fellas. Let's be in here and dressed by 3:30 tomorrow. We'll take the field to loosen up by 3:45."

Coach Spencer signaled for us to hit the showers, and he stood and talked quietly with Coach Jackson. All of us got up and headed to our lockers to slip out of practice togs and take a shower. I hesitated a few moments, but decided to go ahead. I walked over to the coaches, and Spencer looked at me. "What do you want, James?"

"Coach, I've been thinking about a family matter, and, well … I need to ask you something." I glanced at Coach Jackson, and Spencer got the hint.

"Come into the office," he said, nodding at his friend. "We'll let Clyde make sure your buddies don't tear up any gear while they're getting cleaned up!"

He had a twinkle in his eye, and I followed him into the office with its two old captain's chairs, two battered pine desks, and the wide metal cabinet that held baseballs, bats, old gloves, and other gear. I closed the door. Spencer moved behind his desk and looked at me with his steady blue eyes. "There's nothing wrong, is there, James?"

Realizing my concern didn't matter to the team, I felt embarrassed. "Sit down, James," the coach said, studying me as he lowered himself into his creaky chair. "What's goin' on? I've known you for years, and today you're acting strange."

Nodding, I lowered myself into the chair. "Coach, there's something happening at home I'd rather not talk about, but it affects my dad, and all of us, so I …."

"James, is your father in good health?"

I saw worry in his eyes. "He's fine health-wise," I replied, trying to smile. "But he's more or less 'courting' a new woman, and … well, my sister suspects something's not on the up-and-up with the lady, and I do too. I believe I need to do a little checking on her, uh, background."

After staring at me for a long minute, Coach Spencer leaned back. "Listen carefully, James. I know my business, and I care about my players, and about their families. Do *not*, and I repeat, do not say or do anything that might *alienate* your father. Do you understand? He's all you have for a parent, and you and I both know Zeke Baker is *first class*."

"Yessir, I know. But I have this checking to do, and I may have to drive out of town, and if possible, I'd like you to excuse me from the game tomorrow."

Suddenly the room turned as silent as a tomb while Coach Spencer stared at me. Finally, he said, "Okay, James. I'm not gonna penalize you, but here's the deal. You promise me you won't do anything foolish, and you will come and talk to me *before* upsetting your dad."

Slowly the coach stood up and looked at me. "I have to ask: Does this 'checking' *have* to occur tomorrow?"

Listening, it dawned on me that I could do it any day this week. But I really needed to do *something* for mine and my sister's peace of mind. Standing up, I grinned. "Now that you mention it, I could wait …"

Spencer interjected: "Good! In fact, I mean *excellent!*" He smiled. "You put that off for a day or two, young man, and your teammates will appreciate you thinking first about the team!"

We shook hands, and the coach added, "You keep me posted, James. Remember, your dad is my friend. By the way, take these gasoline coupons. My wife and I won't need them this week."

He smiled, and a surge of emotion hit me like an electric shock. My eyes watered, but I blinked back the tears. Quietly I thanked him, took the coupons, shoved them in my pocket, and hurried out to join my friends, who were in the showers.

Pulling off my practice clothes, I grabbed a towel from the bench, wrapped it around me, and padded into the concrete-walled shower room with its ten shower heads. In the steamy room, Herb and Jack and Scott and Walt and several others were getting doused. All the while they were making wise cracks, laughing at jokes, splashing water at each other, and washing themselves. Not surprisingly, Herb was popping the younger guys with his towel. I slipped into the fun, and

Herb, spotting me, snapped me a good one. The showers felt great!

II

My classes on Tuesday went smoothly. In the morning, Miss DeRoche explained the steps to take in writing the required paper for English. She also passed sets of two mimeographed pages down each aisle. Herb took them from me and muttered, "You're gonna help me later, right?"

Over my shoulder I whispered, "Yeah," and Herb passed the remaining pages back to Sandy Brown, the studious daughter of Doctor Brown. I glanced back and saw Sandy whispering to her quiet friend behind her, Anna Lynn. Most of the guys and girls I know in English are learning to write good essays, but you have to keep on writing to improve.

After the lunch hour, I headed for room 103 for Geometry with Miss Martin. When I took my seat a minute before 1:00, she was writing linear equations on the blackboard. Most of the guys and girls I know in this class are having trouble calculating the equations correctly.

On a funny note, Miss Martin usually makes the chalk squeak when she starts writing on the blackboard, and I'm sure she does it to grab our attention. Smiling, she proceeds to solve the equation, but without squeaking the chalk. She's pretty clever. Today nobody asked questions, so she passed out a mimeographed page of problems for us to solve and turn in tomorrow. Listening to her explain, I gazed at the blackboard thinking about baseball and girls until the bell rang.

At 2:00 upstairs in room 212, I have Geography. Mister Knudson, who mainly teaches History, likes having us draw maps of different parts of America. A week ago he told us that President Roosevelt has a family estate called Hyde Park on the Hudson River in upstate New York. "FDR," as most people call him, recently spent a weekend at the Hyde Park estate, and Knudson brought along copies of newspaper clippings to show us.

Mister Knudson also loves teaching about the federal jobs programs the President backs, and how those programs operate to reduce unemployment across America. In fact, last year the need for more wartime spending led to the end of his favorite, the Civilian Conservation Corps. The CCC, as the agency was called, hired thousands of young men, mostly aged 18-25, to work on conservation projects like planting trees, making trails, and improving state and national parks. Today when the bell rang, I hated leaving.

Once in the hall, I thought about how we need to play a good game today against Waynesboro to keep our winning streak alive. A few moments later I saw Herb coming from study hall. Descending the staircase together, we hurried along the back hall to the boy's locker room. On the way we ran into Jack Jones, Scott Matthews, Walt Bunker, and Dave Pankavich.

Taking a look through one of the tall windows lining the hall, I saw the sun shining brightly. We have reached early summer, and the weather is warm enough for short sleeves. Everyone knows it can be hot and sticky in Charlottesville in the summer, but we have great baseball weather in May and June.

In the locker room, I noticed Coach Spencer posted the lineup. He and Coach Jackson were standing outside their office talking over game strategy for Waynesboro, but everyone knows on game day you change and put on the uniforms in a hurry. By 3:30, all of us were sitting on the side bench waiting for the "pep talk." Today, the coach mentioned a couple of their big hitters, but mainly he spoke about Waynesboro's star right-hander, Charley Gondol.

Coach Jackson stood behind Spencer, arms crossed over his chest, but Spencer does the talking before a game. "Listen up, you guys … this Gondol fella is a senior heading for Duke University on a baseball scholarship. We heard the catcher, Dick Wright, is going with Gondol."

Spencer looked around. "Okay, the key to Gondol's success for three years of high school as well as summer league baseball is a really *good* curveball, and I mean *good*. He can break the curve high, low, inside, or outside, and he doesn't always throw the pitch at the same speed. He's got a good fastball, but you're *not* gonna see it with two strikes."

Ten minutes later, we were warming up, and fifteen minutes after that, we took the field. Walt Bunker took his last warmup pitch, and Mister Bronston, the umpire, yelled "Play ball!"

Walt looked nervous, and facing the leadoff batter, a right-handed hitter, he ran the count to 3-0. Herb took a timeout and trotted out to calm him down. When play resumed, Walt fired a fastball down the middle, and the tall sandy-haired outfielder doubled to deep left center.

For the rest of the first inning, Walt looked shaky. After two walks and two more hits, Waynesboro led, 3-0. Walt finally retired the side, after giving up a third base on balls.

In our half of the first, we saw Gondol's curveball. Surprisingly, Jack Jones, a left-handed hitter, struck out swinging. On the bench afterward, he was mumbling. Scooter Thornton, a right-handed hitter, took strike three watching a curve that broke nearly *two feet*. He came back to the bench shaking his head.

As the third batter, I took strike one on a low curveball. The second one broke at the knees, and I swung over it. The third pitch was a fastball in on my hands, and Bronston said "Ball one!" The next bender looked low, but I fouled it off to the right. Gondol's best curveball caught me looking as the ball seemed to curve inside. Raising his right arm, Bronston said "Strike three."

Feeling bad, I trotted toward the bench, Scott Matthews tossed me my first baseman's glove, and I trotted out to my position. While I was tossing grounders to our infielders, I realized Gondol's last curveball broke *toward* me, not away.

Waynesboro looked good. For the top of the second, Coach Spencer switched Scott from third base to pitcher, and Walt moved over to play third. Fortunately for Jefferson, Scott had good stuff, and he struck out the side. But in the bottom of the second, Gondol struck out Herb Jenkowski, one of our best hitters, Bob James, the right fielder, and Scott grounded to first for the third out.

It went like that for four more innings. Gondol struck out two or three of our guys on an assortment of curveballs that hardly anyone could believe. He could throw every kind of curve, including a slight reverse curve.

After the fourth inning, when I mentioned that to Herb as he strapped on the shin guards, he looked at me and nodded. "James, the first time I saw that pitch was last summer when my dad took me and Jack to see the Washington Senators. We had seats a few rows up behind home plate. We could see the pitcher's fastball moving faster and the curveballs really breaking. Dad called the pitch a 'slider.' Instead of breaking where you expect, it's like a reverse curve that moves the opposite way a few inches."

Coach Spencer heard Herb. "That's what I thought," he said quietly. "That's a major league pitch. A right-handed pitcher normally twists his wrist counter clockwise as he releases the pitch, but if he's throwing a slider, he'll twist the wrist a little clockwise. It gives the ball a reverse spin, and the ball moves in the direction it's spinning. You're seeing why this guy Gondol is tough."

Fortunately for us, Scott had his curveball and fastball working, although I think our guys were wondering if he would get tired and lose his control. In the top of the seventh, Scott induced the first two batters to ground out. The third guy, the redheaded first baseman, doubled off the fence in right center.

Coach Spencer yelled "*Baker*!" Walking out to the pitcher's box, he waved me over. "James, you're gonna pitch, Scott, you're going back to third, and Walt, you're on the bench."

Turning, he signaled to Coach Jackson for the changes. Jackson sent John Kilpatrick, the speedy tenth grader, out to left field, and Jack Jones, watching, raised his hands as if to say *What's happening?* I figured the coach was taking him out. After his third straight strikeout in the fifth inning, Jack had flung his bat toward our bench, but luckily it missed everyone.

Waving him to the pitcher's box, Coach Spencer turned his back to me and Herb and spoke into Jack's ear. He listened, frowned, and trotted over to first base. I had never seen Jack play first base before, but he's an excellent player, and versatile, too. Facing me, the coach said quietly, "Save your drop ball for last. Don't show these guys your best pitch too soon … *Get me*?"

I nodded, and Herb nodded, and without a word he returned to his position behind home plate. Coach Spencer headed for the bench, and Mister Bronston let me throw a few warmup pitches. When I was ready, I put my left foot on the pitcher's board, and Bronston yelled "Play ball!"

The batter was right-handed, a guy with a guy with broad shoulders who already rapped two singles. He took his stance, swishing his bat a few times. Herb looked out and held down two fingers. Taking the stretch position, I threw a hard curve, which the batter swung and missed for strike one. Taking the stretch, I checked the base runner, and again Herb called for the curve. I threw another bender, but this one looked low.

"Strike two!" yelled Mister Bronston, and our fans started clapping. Herb tossed me the ball. I gloved it, bowed my head, and said a prayer. I knew what I had to do.

Next, Herb waggled three fingers, and I took the stretch. I hurled a good drop, the big-shouldered hitter made a picture perfect swing, but he just bounced the ball toward third base. Just before reaching the base, the ball went foul. Scott gloved the ball and tossed it back to me. Getting ready, I wondered *Did I release that ball wrong*?

I figured Herb would call for a curveball, but as I looked at his eyes behind the catcher's mask, he put down three fingers and flicked them. *Drop ball.*

I trusted Herb. Taking a deep breath, I threw the pitch, really twisting my wrist as I released the ball. It spun forward nicely, and near the plate it dropped sharply. Watching it, the batter swung right through that baseball! Bronston yelled "*Strike three!*"

We ran off the field like a fire might catch up with us! Waynesboro still led, 3-0, and Gondol came out and took warmups, smiling like we were doomed. During that last inning, Coach Spencer spoke to each of us as we went up to bat. His advice was simple: "Move up half a step closer to Gondol, and swing a little early at his curve. Hit his curve *before* the big break!"

Herb came up first, took his stance, and lined the first curveball into center for a single. After that, Gondol worked from the stretch position. Bob connected with the first curve, and he banged the ball to left center for a double, and Herb raced around to score. Now we trailed, 3-1.

Scott singled to left on the first pitch, and Bob scored, cutting Waynesboro's lead to 3-2. Kilpatrick came up to bat looking nervous. But Coach Spencer had Gondol's pitching figured, and later we heard the coach told John to keep taking until he had two strikes. He took five pitches in a row, and he walked.

Gondol must have been tiring. Jefferson had runners on first and second, and Damon Vann singled on a two-strike curve, tying the score at 3-3 and leaving runners on first and second. By now the crowd was excited. Most of them were clapping in rhythm, stomping the bleachers, and yelling for a hit!

Stepping to the plate, Jack took a wider stance, but he swung and missed the first curveball. He looked at our bench, and Coach Spencer gave him a signal. Jack nodded. I watched him move into his stance, cock his bat, and stare at Gondol. Taking his stretch, Charley hurled another curve. Just before he released the ball, Jack moved up a half step. Keeping his eye on the curve breaking in toward him, he swung level, and *crack*!

Jones belted that curve as hard as anyone I ever saw hit a baseball! Kneeling with my bat in the on-deck circle, I came to my feet like a jack-in-the-box! On our bench the hit caused our guys to react like me, and everyone rose like the soaring ball yanked them to their feet. Coach Spencer gazed open-mouthed as that ball rocketed high into center field and finally landed far beyond the fence!

By then we were jumping up and down, yelling, clapping, and celebrating! I glanced over at the bleachers and saw my friends yelling and clapping. At the end of the bleachers I spotted my father. He had the biggest smile I've ever seen on his face!

I know my memory of the battle of curveballs will last forever. And that game will remain the time at Jefferson High when Jack Jones redeemed himself for throwing his bat. What a day!

III

On Wednesday morning I drove Nat to school in the pickup. Fortunately, we arrived in the parking lot early enough for me to pull in and turn around easily. Nat glanced at me a few times on the way, maybe because I didn't say much about what I had in mind for today. Climbing out with her books, she looked at me in the driver's seat, and I grinned.

"Listen, Sis. I've got a little personal business to take care of today, and if all goes well, I'll have some new information about Missus LaSalle, probably after dinner."

"So you've got something to do, and I need to 'cover' for you. You're dusting off your 'Teen Spies' skills, right?" Her eyes gleamed. "That's fine with me, Big Brother!"

I grinned. "I suppose that's the idea. But like last year, you and I *will* figure out this new mystery."

Giving me a knowing smile, she turned and hurried toward the entrance. Turning the truck around, I drove out of town bound for Roanoke. When I reached Route 250, a two-lane paved road, I glanced at my watch. It was 8:45. I turned west on the highway traveling over Afton Mountain and across the Shenandoah Valley. The day was bright, the sky clear, and a light breeze was blowing. I made good time by averaging 50 miles per hour.

Regardless, I drove steadily. I kept thinking over Coach Spencer's advice about Dad, the details of yesterday's game, and what I hoped to find out about Missus LaSalle. After nearly one hour, I slowed for the City Limits of Staunton. In the middle of town I turned south on US-11, the two-lane highway angling from upper New York through Staunton and Roanoke all the way to Mississippi. A sign announced Woodrow Wilson, the 28th President, was born in Staunton.

At a traffic signal, I rolled both windows down. When the light turned and I drove ahead, the air moving in the truck kept me refreshed. While I motored along, I had plenty of time to think.

Nat and I could no longer believe Dad wanted a romantic relationship with Aunt Cora. During the last three weeks, he "dated" Helen LaSalle twice that we knew about. After Sunday's church service, he surprised us by inviting the lady and her daughter to our home for lunch. Regarding Dad's personal life, we understood the time would arrive when he likely would marry again. We also realized he knew enough about life to make a good choice.

The longer I drove, the more I thought about Missus LaSalle. She told Dad she came from Roanoke, so that seemed like a good starting point. I figured the city would have a public library where I hoped to find some old newspapers, magazines and or books that could help me learn more about an attractive black-haired woman and her little girl with two first names. When I had to explain where I had gone on a school day, I decided to tell the truth and let the chips fall. Dad always says honesty is the best policy.

After passing an intersection with a sign pointing west to Fincastle, I saw a mileage sign saying 15 miles to Roanoke. Thirty minutes later, after following US-11 all the way downtown, I turned onto Jefferson Street. Stopping at an intersection, I asked a teenage girl in a blue dress if she knew where the city library was located. Smiling, she pointed to an old two-story mansion ahead on the left. Parking at the curb, I climbed out and stretched. Crossing the street, I followed a walkway past a Roanoke Library sign to Elmwood Park.

Entering the building, I spotted the circulation desk. A tall woman in a gray dress with a bouffant blonde hairdo gazed at me with curious brown eyes. "Can I help you, young man?"

Having thought my reply to that very question, I smiled. "Yes, Ma'am. We have an aunt and uncle who lived in Roanoke for several years, until recently, and my cousin wants help in researching the family history."

"Hmm … I *see*." Studying me like I was a character of dubious repute, she rolled her eyes and pointed to a wide staircase. "You need to go downstairs to where we house the archives. The library has the city's old newspapers, all properly arranged."

Thanking her, I headed down the old stairs. The basement turned out to be a large brightly lighted room with several rows of shelves holding books. I also saw wider shelves at the walls that held old newspapers, magazines, and scrapbooks as well as large covered boxes with content information printed on the ends. A faintly unused smell greeted me as if I was one of the few people who ever paid the room a visit.

Behind a wooden desk stood a trim forty-something woman dressed in a starched white blouse and a blue "victory suit." She wore her black hair in the Pageboy style. As I stepped up to the desk, she gazed at me through black plastic-rimmed glasses that made her blue eyes look larger. The brass plaque on the desk said *Miss V. Garst, Archives*.

I smiled politely. "My name is James Baker, and I have an unusual request."

"Of course," Miss Garst replied. "So do most people who come to the archives." I saw the flicker of a smile as she studied me like a book to be cataloged. "Follow me."

She led me to the right wall where newspapers bound into three-month bundles had been sorted and stored on wide shelves. Listening to her, I realized she must have spent countless hours creating a name index on 3x5 cards for each day's newspapers, notably the *Roanoke Times*, the morning paper, and the *Roanoke World-News*, the evening paper. All those years worth of information had been stored in a five-foot varnished pine card catalog with two dozen drawers.

Nodding, she returned to her desk, and I began with the card catalog. Searching for the name "LaSalle, Helen," I was surprised to come across a card referring to an obituary dated March 10, 1926, from the *World-News*. I pulled from the shelf the bundle of newspapers containing that issue, blew the dust off, and several minutes later I found a small obit without a picture, but it did mention Helen LaSalle had graduated from James Monroe High in June of 1926.

At that moment I realized except for two pencils, I was unprepared for research. I returned to Miss Garst, and she offered a smile along with a small notebook to record my findings.

"By the way, James," and her eyes studied me again. "You might be interested to know we have a full run of the yearbooks of each city high school." Warming up to the task, she pointed me to the opposite wall and a large wooden bookcase loaded with yearbooks. "If you have any questions, just ask." This time her smile lingered.

She knows her stuff I thought. At the bookcase, I looked at the yearbooks until I found Monroe High's 1926 *Chronicle*. Paging through it, I found the senior picture of Helen LaSalle, and I did a double take. Not only was she not the woman our father knows, but a ribbon of black surrounded her picture. Beside her name under the picture, I read "1908-1926. Beloved by All."

After reflecting on what to do, I looked carefully at the pictures of all two dozen seniors. In a few moments I saw the face of the Helen we know, smiling in a black-and-white photo. But the name underneath was the name Abigail Evans. My eyes widened as I stared at the sepia photograph.

Shelving the yearbook, I returned to the card catalog and looked up "Evans, Abigail." The only card I found said "Wedding to fellow Roanoker Ralph Beverly Shaw," and it listed a 1933 article that presumably covered the wedding. So I thought *Her married name must be Abigail Shaw.*

Looking up "Shaw, Abigail" in the card catalog, I found a card that eventually led me to a 7-year old newspaper article about a court trial. The story reported Abigail Shaw was convicted for embezzling $5,300 from an unnamed church where she worked as secretary for three years.

Abigail was sentenced to three years in prison, despite being pregnant and claiming her husband Ralph Shaw beat her repeatedly. She stated the money was needed to escape and start a new life. After the trial, the husband told reporters he would claim the baby after it was born in prison.

I stood there with the new information spinning like a top in my mind. After taking notes of all I had learned, I returned to the desk and thanked Miss Garst. This time she smiled warmly, and her blue eyes seemed to dance. She held my hand a little longer after we shook hands while she peered into my eyes. "Now, James, if you ever have any questions with which the library archives can help, please, come back and *see me.*"

Smiling at her, I turned toward the stairs. A middle aged man about my height with dark hair and a mustache was descending the stairs. As I reached the staircase, the handsome newcomer, who looked like a movie character out of a smoky café somewhere, passed me. Climbing the stairs, I heard Miss Garst's voice from the desk: "Harry, you look hale and hearty today! What do you plan to research?"

"Nothing" came the masculine reply. "I've started writing. I thought you could join me for a cup of coffee in a local bistro … and maybe, well, take a long walk in the park."

Continuing to the main floor, I walked out the door into the sunshine. Smiling about the scene downstairs, I strolled toward the pickup thinking *I need to figure out what to say to Dad.*

IV

As I crossed Jefferson Street, I noticed an old trolley car converted to a 24-hour diner on my left. My watch said 1:15. Suddenly I felt hungry, and I walked the short distance to the Elmwood Diner. Just as I climbed the two steps at the diner's silver door, two young women wearing colorful dresses and a little boy in a sailor outfit came out the door. Stopping, the second woman smiled at me and held it open. Returning the smile, I entered.

The mixed aromas of coffee, baked bread, and fried bacon greeted me. At first glance the customers, men, women, and a few kids, could have been dressed to go to church. Most of the men wore suits, and the women wore dresses. Some topped their outfits with the kind of hats women often wear on Sundays. It pleased me that I had thought to wear my new blue shirt and my khaki trousers along with my black shoes.

A tall balding waiter with dark eyes and a wide grin saw me. Attired in a white shirt with a black bow tie along with dark trousers, he hurried over. "Welcome, young man, to the finest diner in town!" I saw a name tag for Henry above his shirt pocket. "Do you have a lady companion?"

"I don't, but the sign out front says you serve everything from dinners to snacks. I'd like to get a hamburger and coffee before I head for home."

Bowing, he led me to a small table at the far end of the onetime trolley. I slid into the cushioned seat, and he made a note on his pad. "Can I get you anything else, sir?"

I leaned forward. "Do you mind telling me if you're from Roanoke?"

He looked at me with suspicious eyes. "Yes, sir, I am. But why do you ask?"

I explained about my research on a family that once lived there. "The name that kept showing up in old clippings was Abigail Shaw …"

Leaning forward, Henry wiped the table with his small towel. Without looking at me, he said quietly, "Yes, sir, the Shaw woman. It's been years ago now, but a story about her did appear in the papers. Most folks kept mum about it, but I heard she ended up in prison for a while. They say something went wrong at her job …"

Standing upright, he gave me a knowing look, turned, and headed for the window ledge of the kitchen. A dark-faced cook looked out. Taking the order slip, he disappeared into the kitchen. All the while the diner teemed with activity, and the buzz of conversation filled the air.

In a few minutes Henry appeared with a hamburger and French fries on a white plate next to a heavy white mug. He left a tab by my elbow, and I proceeded to make fast work of my lunch. As I ate and sipped coffee, I wondered about what my friends were doing at school.

I finished the coffee. In a few moments Henry returned, leaned over, and said, again in a quiet voice,

"Sir, if you like, you can pay me instead of waiting at the cash register."

Glancing toward the register, I saw three young men waiting in line behind two older men outfitted in blue uniforms with black-brimmed blue caps. I couldn't see the name on the cap, but Roanoke is known as home to the Norfolk and Western Railroad, and the rail yards couldn't be far away. I took the pair as conductors, and they were chatting with the pretty red-headed cashier

I handed Henry the slip along with the .45 cents for the lunch and a 15 cents for the tip. Thanking me with a wide smile, he headed for two waiting customers. I walked out and back to the truck. Slipping into the front seat and starting the engine, I motored past the stately Hotel Roanoke. Turning onto US-11, I drove a few blocks.

Near the city limits, I stopped at a Friendly Service Station. Like so many filling stations, the flat building was painted white and topped by a red roof. I waited for two cars ahead of me, a beaten-up black Ford and a prewar maroon Dodge. Two attendants, both attired in gray cotton uniforms with peaked caps, were handling the job.

When my turn came, I pulled up beside the double pumps topped by red globes labeled *Friendly*. The smiling attendant at my window had Ken above his white shirt pocket. "Fill her up?"

I said yes, and he asked for my coupons. I produced two coupons given to me by Coach Spencer. Ken went to the pump, cranked the handle, and pumped the gasoline. Douglas, his partner, came to the window. "Check your oil, sir?"

Nodding, I watched him. I climbed out and walked around to the men's rest room on the building's left side. By the time I returned, Ken told me the charge was $3.22, and I paid him while Douglas finished washing the windshield. The entire job took no more than 4-5 minutes.

Starting the motor, I drove off the premises and on US-11 on my way to Charlottesville. I had to needed to be home before dinner, so I kept the speed close to 50. I had plenty of thinking to do. Unknown to our family, I was about to affect the course of Dad's interest in "Helen LaSalle." I also wondered if I could do anything about Nat's growing interest in Ernie Herbert.

When I reached home, I would have to share with Nat what I had found with the help of a bright archivist at Roanoke's city library. At the same time, the more I knew about Ernie, the more I wondered what I didn't know.

Chapter 8

Step by Step

I pulled into our driveway well before dinner on that Wednesday. Breathing a sigh of relief, I parked the truck in its usual place behind the barn. Climbing out slowly, I yawned and stretched. Hearing one of our horses whinnying in the barn made me think horses might have the same sense that dogs have, being able to tell when a family member comes home.

I walked toward the house, and Nat stepped out the back door and waved. Looking cheerful, she hurried to greet me. She hugged me, and I gave her a big squeeze. "What's up, Sis? Did you really *miss* me?"

"I guess so, but I kept hoping all would go smoothly."

Her familiar oval face, greenish-brown eyes, and eager personality reminded me of our mother, and I smiled. "I'm going to take care of some chores before dinner. You and I can talk later tonight when we're doing homework."

"Did you uncover anything worthwhile?"

"Yes, I did, but the situation's more complicated than we thought." I rolled my eyes. "Anyway, I'm going to change into something more casual, and then I'll work in the garden."

She squeezed my hand. "I think Aunt Cora and Dad figure you went to baseball practice, so you'll know how to handle that." Her eyes sparkled as we strolled into the kitchen. Aunt Cora saw me and smiled. "Well, there you are, James. I hope your day has been a good one."

I returned her smile. "So far, so good. I'm going to do a little hoeing after I change out of my school clothes."

"Your father had to run an errand in town, but I'm sure he'll be back before dinner."

I nodded, and Nat led the way to the dining room and up the stairs. In the hallway, she turned to me. "Mister Bronston talked a lot about World War I today, and it was interesting. I never realized the English and the French were fighting the Germans for *three full years* before President Wilson asked Congress to declare war in 1917. I guess I need to reread that chapter."

She headed for her room at the end of the hall, and I went into my room, closing the door. I changed from my school clothes to a pair of jeans, a blue work shirt, and my older shoes. As I walked out to the garden, I wondered what "errand" took our father to town in mid-afternoon.

II

D ad arrived home just before 6:00, and dinner started on time. Today Aunt Cora prepared pork chops, sweet potatoes, green beans, and iced tea. We also had a slice of rye bread with margarine instead of butter. For dessert she made bread pudding, which is a real treat!

Again I realized Aunt Cora meant much more to us than her cooking, cleaning, and being a confidante, not to mention her upbeat personality. She was more like a mother than an aunt. The longer we know her, the closer she comes to being our mom. Maybe she feels like the Lord gave her a second chance at a family. Whatever the reasons, she seems content to be here and help us.

After dinner, Dad said he would help Aunt Cora do the dishes. I noticed he had taken over this chore on a regular basis, so he must feel closer to her in more ways than one. For example, on Sunday evenings they often listen to the same radio program together.

Nat observed that she had to study for Mister Bronston and World History. She went upstairs, and I started to follow, but Dad said, "Hang on, James. I have something to show you."

Indicating the den, he led me into his sanctuary. Once inside, he strolled over to the oak curio case. Beside it stood a new bat. He picked it up, stepped back, gripped the handle near the knob, and took a few slow practice swings.

"Try this, James, and see if you like it."

Caught off guard, I couldn't speak. He handed me the bat, and taking it, I moved into the center of the room. Like Dad, I gripped the bat and swung it slowly a few times. I noticed the trademark burned into the barrel of the bat: Hillerich and Bradsby, a famous American bat company.

I had to smile. "This feels about right …"

"Good, James. I'll keep the receipt just in case. I gave you one of my northern ash bats, but later it occurred to me that you might prefer a new one."

He grinned. "You will notice it's a Ted Williams model, and they say Ted swings 33 or 34 ounce bats. He says you get a quicker swing with a smaller bat, and that causes more *impact* on the baseball. No matter. It really depends on how *you think* it feels after your next game."

"Geez, Dad, I had no idea …"

"Well, we can talk about bats later. I need to help Cora before she washes all those dishes!"

I started to thank him, but he left headed for the kitchen. I grinned, took the bat, and went upstairs to my room. There for a minute or two my eyes felt teary, but as I wiped them, I heard Nat's voice behind me. "You have some news, Big Brother, so let's hear it."

Blinking away the tears, I turned around.

"Dad got you a new bat, eh? That looks like a beauty!"

We smiled at each other, and I shifted gears. "Have a seat, Sis, and I'll tell you the essence of what I found." Closing the door, I sat on the side of the bed facing her.

"First, the drive wasn't bad at all. I talked to Coach Spencer on Monday about making a trip to check on a personal matter, and I told him Dad was 'courting' a woman. I wasn't specific, but Spencer made me promise not to say or do anything that would really upset Dad."

I looked at her. "Well, I promised, and I won't. The coach is right. We shouldn't do anything so drastic as to upset our father, especially when he's our only parent."

"That's what Mister Spencer said?"

I nodded. "Going back to Missus Helen LaSalle, I'll summarize what she told Dad. First, she said that her husband died, and she's raising little Joyce on her own. I understand that she told him she was born and raised in Roanoke, graduated from Monroe High, worked as a waitress in town, and married a local man. They were married three years, and she had Joyce, who's now six years old. Helen also said a couple of weeks after the baby was born, her husband left her. She worked part-time jobs until she found the church secretary's position, but I don't think she mentioned the church's name."

I studied Nat. "Are you with me?" When she nodded, I continued: "We know the background from Dad is secondhand, because he presumes all that she tells him is true. But maybe not."

Sighing, I added, "Further, the minister in Roanoke sympathized with her, and so he hired her. Probably a committee was involved, but you know they're going to choose the person a minister favors for a job in a church, particularly for his secretary. So far her story is all plausible."

My sister nodded, and I moved ahead. "This is where the city library proved useful. The archivist in the Roanoke library, Miss Garst, has organized an entire card catalog covering information that appeared in the local newspapers and magazines. She showed me how to use it, and later she helped me find something. Here's the main point. The woman we know is Abigail Shaw, not Helen LaSalle."

I eyed Nat as her mouth dropped open. Staring at me, she said. "You're not *kidding*, are you?"

"Nope, but get this. When I looked up Helen LaSalle in the 1926 yearbook for Monroe High, the picture showed Helen LaSalle *died* in 1926. To me that means the woman Dad knows 'borrowed' the name, probably when she moved to Charlottesville with Joyce. That explains why the girl we know as Joyce told you her name in Roanoke was *Janet*."

Nat's eyes virtually bulged open, and I paused. "Hang on, Sis. Realizing that, I had an idea. I looked through all of the pictures of the seniors in that '26 yearbook, and I found the picture of the woman we know as Helen LaSalle was really *Abigail Evans*. Looking up Abigail Evans in the card catalog, a card said she had married 'fellow Roanoker Ralph Beverly Shaw. Under the name 'Shaw, Abigail,' I eventually got pointed to an article saying that Abigail Shaw was convicted of embezzling more than $5,000 from the church where she worked. Despite being pregnant, she was tried, convicted, and sentenced to three years in prison. The husband told reporters he planned to take the baby after it was born in prison."

Nat stared at me with her eyes wide open, and in a few seconds she said, "James! If all of that is correct, it means *nothing* we were told about the so-called Helen LaSalle is true!"

I nodded. "Yeah, that's what I concluded. Further, I figure she kidnapped her own child after she got out of prison. Maybe the husband did get custody of the child, but most likely his wife, or his mother, took care of the baby. So if Abigail did kidnap the child, it's no wonder she had to change her identity when she took off for Charlottesville. The authorities might still be looking for her.

Nat took several deep breaths as she digested what I told her. Finally, her voice low, she asked, "Okay, now what?"

"I'm thinking about what's next, but I'm not ready to tell Dad."

She rubbed her eyes. "That's good. In fact, we should sleep on this information."

Nat stood up. As she turned to leave, I grabbed her arm. "Do not tell any of this to *anyone*."

I stared into her eyes, and her she nodded several times. "Yes, I do understand, James."

Suddenly she embraced me, tightly. I felt her tears on the side of my face. She stepped back looking at me with damp eyes. Slowly my sister turned and left, closing the door after her.

Wiping my forehead with one hand, I felt worn out. I stretched out on the bed looking at the yellowish globe over the light fixture on the ceiling. I wondered who designed the fairy-like orange and blue figures dancing around the globe in some make-believe land.

III

After practice ended around 4:30 on Thursday, everyone headed for the locker room and the showers, but first Coach Spencer seated us on the side bench and gave his pep talk. I was sitting next to Herb, and on the other side, Damon was whispering to Scott. Damon is a quick-handed infielder and a nice guy, and he's usually pretty quiet. When Spencer glared at those guys and cleared his throat, both of them clammed up.

"All right, fellas," the coach said, looking at us. "This year we're riding a new school bus to Western High, in Richmond. We'll get out of classes at 2:00, and we want to be on the road by 2:30, so get to the locker room and change right away. The trip will take an hour and a half, and we hope to start the game by 4:45."

Coach Spencer wiped his forehead. "That's all for today. Take your shower. Go home, have a good night's sleep, and be in uniform by 2:30 tomorrow."

After dismissing us with a wave, Coach Spencer walked over to me. The guys nearby gave us a little room, and Spencer lowered his voice. "James, did you find out what you wanted?"

I nodded once. "Yes, and, well, I found a little background stuff that surprised me."

"Have you spoken to your father about it?"

"Not yet, coach. But I will, after I figure out how to approach him. I'll be careful, like you said."

He winked at me. "Remember, James, if you want someone to talk with who will keep it under his hat, you can come to me."

That afternoon I immersed myself in the warm, steamy, wise-cracking shower scene as much as ever. I think most people believe that being on a ball team and playing a game is mostly about how well you perform and whether your team wins or loses. They don't realize that guys in a school or team organization know each other, practice together, dress and shower together, joke and talk, so the camaraderie that results is a vital part of the game too. Naturally the ball games are the centerpiece, but practices and games by themselves do not explain the intriguing appeal that draws boys onto teams. I imagine the same appeal exists for girls' teams, too.

One thing's for sure. The coach makes a big impact on the team and the players. When push comes to shove, coaches have all played the game when they were younger. They know how to play the game as well as teach the fundamentals. I suppose the problems and situations that arise are similar, but I know having a good coach, or coaches, is one of the best parts of sports.

In our case, Coach Spencer may talk tough sometimes, and he may push us, but you know he'll back you in a crunch. That's almost like having a second father. No doubt a bad coach can have the opposite effect, but so far I've been fortunate to have good coaches.

That afternoon Walt Bunker rode home with me. After showering and dressing, we walked out to the parking lot. We climbed in the pickup, rolled the windows down, and I asked, "Do you want to go for a double date at the movies this weekend? I know you've dated Wanda Winston before."

Nodding, Walt smiled. "I saw in the paper that *Reap the Wild Wind* is playing. It's supposed to be an adventure film featuring really big stars like Ray Milland and John Wayne."

He looked at me. "Did you have a movie in mind?"

"Well, I've read a couple of stories about an Alfred Hitchcock mystery called *Saboteur*. In this film a factory worker, played by Robert Cummings, is accused of sabotage for supposedly setting a fire in a wartime airplane plant. Anyway, Cummings' character travels across the country to clear his name. While he's on the run, he takes a hostage, played by Priscilla Lane, but I think she ends up helping him clear his name. So it's a good mystery, and set in World War II."

I slowed for Walt's house, and he grinned. "Yeah, *Saboteur* does sound pretty good. I'll invite Wanda Winston, and I think she'll go. Will you ask Linda Lawton?"

"Sure. Linda and I had a good time at the movies not too long ago, when we doubled with Herb and Iris at *Casablanc*a."

Stopping in front of the house, I added, "Let's call the girls tonight. That way if one or the other of us needs to call another girl for Saturday, we have time. Dad will let me take the '39 Chevy."

Getting out, Walt agreed. "Well, you saw the black '40 Chevrolet my folks recently bought. I'll ask Dad about driving. That way neither of us will *cramp* the other's style on the way home!"

I grinned as Walt closed the door. He eyed me through the window. "Okay, let me know. We'll figure on seeing the 5:00 or 5:30 show, and afterwards, we can go for a hamburger, and, then …"

He winked, and grinned, and I knew what he meant. "See you tomorrow at school."

I accelerated, and fifteen minutes later, I parked the truck behind the barn. Getting out, I stretched, looked at the sun starting its slide down to the western horizon, and headed for the kitchen.

Chapter 9

Baseball and Movies

On a sunny Friday afternoon, we had to take a bus trip to Richmond to play Western High. For the away games we get dismissed from classes an hour early. Everybody hustles to the locker room, changes into his game uniform, and carries his bat and duffel bag with baseball gear on the bus. Today at 2:35 Ray Riley took the wheel. Steering bus #10 out of the lot, he drove east toward highway 250.

Taking a bus trip to a high school game is an adventure. Everyone but Jack Jones had a seat partner, and Jack brought his English textbook, his notebook, and a couple of ink pens to finish an overdue English paper.

I sat next to Herb Jenkowski, who likes an aisle seat. We sat behind Scott Matthews and Bob James, who had the seats directly behind Coach Jackson on the right side. In a way, a long bus ride is boring, but mostly we talk about the upcoming game and, of course, girls.

After a few miles, Herb said quietly: "I hope Walt has good stuff today, but we'll see. One of these days maybe the coach will try Bob. He's throwing pretty good stuff to me after our practices."

Taking a quick look around, Herb continued: "Bob's a right-hander and a sophomore, but he throws a good curve and a fair fastball. I'm showing him how to change speeds, so he's gonna be more effective than people might think."

Across the aisle and two rows back sat Walt Bunker and Dave Pankavich. Off and on I heard Walt talking to Dave about doing his best each time at bat. Dave is a good fielder with a strong arm, but if a pitcher gets him out the first time, he usually struggles with hitting that day.

When I wasn't talking about baseball or girls with Herb, I could hear other guys talking about different stuff. I listened off and on but mainly looked out the window at the passing countryside. This is May, and everything is blooming. Trees line Route 250 on the way to Richmond, so it's not as scenic as you might think. You see plenty of side roads, various kinds of houses, and the farms usually have a barn, horses or cattle, a tractor or two, and plowed fields planted with crops like corn, wheat, or cotton.

The next thing I knew our players were talking loudly, so I must have dozed off. Ray Riley was steering the bus into a big parking lot with a brick school building on one side and a baseball diamond and football field on the other. The diamond looked a lot like ours: a dirt infield with chalk lines along the first and third base lines, a heavy wire backstop that stood about 20 feet high, and chain link fences that circled the outfield and connected to the backstop.

After the bus was parked, everyone carefully descended the three steps in spikes. Coach Spencer directed us to the visitors bench, covered by an inclined roof, on the first base side. We set down our bats and duffel bags, and the coach said to play "pepper" and loosen up.

Pepper is a practice drill played with a few fielders standing about 10 to 12 feet opposite a player with a bat. A fielder underhands the ball to the batter, and he hits it back on the bounce, a teammate gloves the ball, he tosses it to the batter, and you repeat the action.

After about ten minutes of warming up, Coach Jackson hollered to hit the bench, and we collected there. Already the coaches turned in their lineups to the umpire, who is probably a teacher. We have first at-bats, and Coach Jackson noted the time in our scorebook as 4:15.

Western's pitcher was a tall sandy-haired right-hander named Jeff Blackmon, according to what Herb heard from their catcher. Jack Jones, our leadoff hitter and left fielder, strolled up to the plate. I've never seen him intimidated by a pitcher, and this guy didn't faze him either. Jack took one pitch outside, and on the second pitch he ripped a double to right center. He stopped at second, and Scott Matthews walked up to bat next.

After taking two balls, he looped a single into right field, and Jack scored.

Western's school scoreboard was on a raised platform behind the backstop. The scorekeeper, a stout man in a blue shirt and tan slacks, put up a large black numeral 1 for VISITORS.

We had maybe two dozen Jefferson backers present, but Western probably had 500 students, parents, and teachers scattered through the bleachers. Our fans were yelling and clapping for the batters. But having only a handful of people supporting you at an away game is the way it goes for most high school teams.

Batting in the third slot, I walked up to home plate. Taking my stance, I watched their pitcher. Going into his stretch, he fooled me with a wide-breaking curve at the knees, and I swung and missed. He threw another low curve, I checked my swing, but the umpire yelled "Strike *two!*"

After trying to stare me down, Blackmon took his stretch. I was set, but he threw a dinky curve that slid away as I swung right through it. "*Strike three!*"

Returning to the bench, I sat on the far end. I hate striking out, because it feels like you let the team down. But like the coach says, you have to hang in there. Batting cleanup, Herb slugged a drive into deep right center, and the ball hit the chain link fence on the fly. Scott scored, Herb made it all the way around to third base, and everyone on our bench was clapping, waving, and yelling. The scorekeeper put up 2 for us.

Bob James, hitting fifth, lined the first pitch over second for a single. Herb trotted home, and the scorekeeper changed the number to 3. We congratulated Herb, and he strapped on his catcher's gear.

Blackmon recovered his poise. Dave Pankavich, the center fielder and number six hitter, popped up to shortstop for the second out. Damon, our shortstop, took two curves for balls, and he lined an outside fastball to the first baseman, who gloved it for the third out.

We took the field ahead, 3-0, and Walt trotted out to pitch. Nobody said anything, but I think most of us were surprised by the coach's choice. Walt, who's a good all-around player, has struggled with his pitching this year. He threw a few warmups, and he looked good. Herb got into his crouch back of home plate, with the right knee on the ground.

Western came up to bat, and before the damage ended, they led, 4-3. Walt gave up five singles and one walk to the first seven batters, and he looked discouraged when the inning finally ended on a forceout at second. Coach Spencer talked to Walt for a long minute. Taking him out, Spencer sent John Kilpatrick to play right field and shifted Bob James from right to pitcher.

Bob had pitched batting practice a few times, but every day he's been spending a few minutes throwing pitches to Herb. Kind of a coach in uniform, Herb was helping Bob learn the ropes.

Coach Spencer made a good choice. After Bob became the pitcher, the game stayed even with each team getting a hit or a walk, or both, in every inning, but neither team scored. Finally, in the bottom of the sixth, Western turned two singles, two walks, and a double into three runs.

When we came up for our last bats in the seventh, Western led, 7-3, and the lead seemed huge. Jeff Blackmon had pitched well all afternoon, and he looked strong. When Bob grabbed his bat to lead off, he told Herb, "I gave it my best, but I'll admit, all the pitching kind of wore me out."

At the plate, Bob took a couple of practice swings. Blackmon wound up and threw a fastball down the middle, and Bob lined it off the left center fence for a double. Dave batted next, and with Blackmon pitching from the stretch, Pankavich stroked a fastball for a single to right, and Bob scored easily. The scorekeeper put up a 4 for VISITORS, and Jefferson trailed, 7-4.

Batting next, Damon, who made several slick fielding plays at shortstop, knocked a curveball into left for a single, and Dave flew around to third. Up came Andy Thornton. Pitching from the stretch, Blackmon fired a fastball over for strike one. When he tried two fast ones in a row, Andy bounced a single into right field, and Dave scored, making it 7-5, with Damon racing over to third. John Kilpatrick, looking determined, swung at the first pitch and looped a single into center, Damon scored, and Scooter sped around to third. Now the scoreboard showed Western's lead reduced to one, 7-6.

Jack Jones strolled to the plate, swishing his bat back and forth like a tiger's tail. With Andy at third and John on first, Western's coach called time. He trotted out, spoke to the pitcher, and Blackmon, his head down, nodded. The coach returned to the bench, the pitcher took off his glove, and wiped his forehead on his sleeve. You could tell he was tired.

Ready again, Blackmon took his stretch, and threw a sidearm curve, but Jack timed it perfectly, and slugged that ball high over the right field fence for a 3-run homer! Watching that blast soar high and deep pulled our players up off the bench like a line of jack-in-the boxes! We yelled and waved and jumped around as Jack trotted around the bases, stepped on home, and doffed his cap! Now Jefferson led, 9-7.

Most of the home team's fans remained quiet, and Blackmon looked upset. Still, he mixed wide curves with dinky curves, fooling Scott and me and retiring us on infield grounders. I was drinking water from my thermos when Herb hit a curveball deep to center, but I saw their outfielder make a nice running catch for the third out.

As we started to take the field, Coach Spencer grabbed me by the arm. "Go out there and warm up, James! You're gonna pitch us to victory!"

He turned to Bob. "You play left field, and I'm sending Jones to first base."

I nodded, trotted out to the pitcher's box, took my warmups, and Jack snagged some throws at first base from the infielders. I thought *I really have to hold this two-run lead.*

Blackmon batted first, and so far he had two singles. Herb pulled down his mask, went into his crouch, held up his mitt as the target, and with his right hand lowered one finger for the fastball. I wound up and threw my fast one over the outside corner, but Blackmon slugged the ball off the left center field fence for a double. That really got the crowd yelling and clapping, but it made me more determined to get their side out.

Next came the first baseman, Ron Gustafson, a stocky right-handed batter who had three long fly outs. Herb lowered two fingers for the curveball, and I slipped a strike over the inside corner for strike one. Again Herb signaled curve, and Gustafson popped it above third base, but Scott made an easy catch. One out.

Herb crouched again, and Peter Gibson, another right-handed hitter, eyed me. Herb signaled for a fastball outside. Taking my stretch, I threw a good fastball, and Gibson looped it into short center field for a single. But Pankavich, running at full speed, scooped the ball up and hurled a strike all the way to Herb at home plate, and Blackmon was forced to hold at third base.

Trotting back to the pitcher's box after backing up the throw at third, I looked around. Western had runners at first and third with one out. I thought *If I throw a good one, maybe we can make a double play*.

Herb had the same thought, because he called time, took off his mask, and trotted out. "James, buddy, keep your *cool*. We can get out of this jam."

Herb looked around when Coach Spencer yelled, "James, you can *do it*! Use your *good stuff*!"

Understanding, Herb faced me. "Spencer means give 'em the *drop ball*. We gotta have a *double play*! Make this pitch *really good*!"

He trotted back to his position, pulled on the mask, crouched, and held up his mitt. The umpire adjusted his mask, and leaned forward behind Herb. For a fleeting moment the batter, the catcher, and the umpire looked like a scene painted by Norman Rockwell.

The hitter, Jason Junker, a short guy who played second base, choked up on the bat. Herb lowered his right hand and moved three fingers for the drop ball. I took my stretch, looked, and broke off a drop that really fell at the end. "*Ball one*!"

Herb called time, stood up, and spoke quietly to the umpire. The slender red-headed fellow removed his mask, stuck out his chin, and yelled "It was *low*, bub! Don't ask questions!"

Pulling on the mask, Herb crouched and again stuck down three fingers, but this time he lifted his mitt higher. The higher target meant to start the drop chest high, and I hurled a good one. The batter saw it coming above the waist, but when he swung, the pitch had dropped, and he bounced a one-hopper to third. Snagging the ball, Scott fired a bullet to Scooter at second. Andy made the play, and sidearmed a throw that bounced once, but Jack scooped it like a major leaguer for the game-ending third out!

Everyone on our team rushed on the field, yelling, clapping me on the back, and congratulating each other! The burst of joy excited me, but in a few moments we all headed off the field. Coach Spencer hugged me, hugged Andy, and turned to Herb. "You big bruiser, you knew what I meant by 'best stuff,' and James, you threw it! Scott, Andy, and Jack, what a *double play*!"

Within twenty minutes, we had boarded the bus with all our equipment. Coach Spencer stood in front beside

Ray Riley at the wheel. "Listen up, you guys! Coach Jackson is gonna come around with a Coca-Cola for all of you. Try not to spill it. On the way we'll find a diner where we can go inside, use the facilities, and buy something to bring on the bus and eat going home."

Coach Spencer sat down next to Coach Jackson, and Mister Riley drove the bus out of the parking lot and followed the road signs to Route 250. We all had a bottle of Coke, and the mood was lighthearted. Ten minutes later, the bus parked in front of a diner called Polly's Eats.

Inside, we sat on stools at the counter. Here we were, a bunch of sweaty, grinning, hungry high school guys in baseball uniforms and stocking feet. Two teenage waitresses, a redhead and a blonde, both wearing blue dresses and white sailor's caps, smiled, kidded us, and took our carry-out orders. The dark-faced cook grinned at us from behind the kitchen ledge. He looked pleased to see the happy customers. The players ordered either a hamburger or a sandwich, and the coaches got hamburgers with all the trimmings.

At the cash register, Coach Spencer bought several bags of potato chips. Everyone returned to the bus, and two minutes later, Ray Riley was turning west on Route 250. We had a fun time eating, sipping a new Coca-Cola, laughing, talking, and making weekend plans.

By the time we climbed off the bus at Jefferson and traipsed to the locker room for a shower, it was nearly 7:00. I was worn out, and I think all the guys felt likewise. But today gave us a memorable experience: the trip, the game, the victory, and the fun of being together. I couldn't wait to tell Dad about our clutch win!

II

On Saturday morning I climbed slowly out of bed shortly after 8:00. Aunt Cora made the four of us a hearty breakfast of fried eggs, sausage, buttered toast, and coffee, and she opened a jar of her own strawberry jam. While we ate, Dad asked me to tell the highlights of the game, especially my pitching. As Nat and I know, he was a star pitcher as a young man.

"The main pitches I relied on," he observed, with a smile, "were the fastball, and I had pretty good control of it, and two kinds of curveballs, one overhand and the other sidearm. My sidearm curve used to break down, James, but not as much as your drop. I liked playing the outfield too, and believe it or not, I could run fast enough to play center field!"

We exchanged a few experiences, and Aunt Cora and Nat seemed fascinated. At one point my sister remarked, "I've had lots of fun watching Jefferson's games. I can't wait to see the next one!"

After breakfast, Dad helped Aunt Cora wash the dishes, and she asked him to tell her more about his ballplaying years. I could tell from his expression that he felt flattered. Later, the two of them went into the living room, relaxed, and exchanged coming-of-age experiences.

I spent a couple of hours hoeing and weeding the garden. When I looked around at what we planted, I figured, barring terrible weather, that we would see good yields of sweet corn, green peas, zucchini squash, tomatoes, and sweet potatoes. We had one acre of white potatoes, an acre of field corn for the horses, and we had 30 acres of wheat to be reaped and sold.

Nat helped with the garden, and later we walked around and looked at our orchards. This was the first week of May, and while I like the apple blossoms, they were falling off. The Albemarle Pippins, Virginia Whites, and Red Delicious apples seemed to be thriving. Next week I would help Dad spray the apple trees, my least favorite chore.

On the way inside for lunch, Nat observed, "I think Dad's stories about playing baseball are really neat. You've said this once, but I can tell he's being modest when he talks about his accomplishments. I'm proud to have a father who's such a stand-up man. These days when I think about him dating Missus LaSalle, well, I just hope he's making a smart choice."

"Look, Nat. I'm sure you've noticed that Dad is spending a fair amount of time with Aunt Cora, too. He's not obvious about it, but I think he's feeling more affection for her. He treats her with great respect, and I think she's a really good woman to have living with us."

Nodding, she changed the subject. "By the way, Big Brother. I have a date this afternoon with Ernie Herbert. Later, I'll let you know how it goes."

We went inside and enjoyed Aunt Cora's ham sandwiches, fried potatoes, coffee, and apples. Later, I spent more than an hour reading a few chapters of *Final Secret*, an intriguing novel by Mickey Mathews. The book is filled with clever fictional characters, but they live through the actual events leading up to the Japanese bombing of Pearl Harbor on December 7, 1941.

Mathews has a way of bringing his characters alive, notably Frank Tuttle, his new friend and a retired Army Major, and Nisei characters like Henry Fujiwaka and Dickie Makumo. Mathews describes places like Pearl Harbor so well that you feel like you're there. Earlier, I asked Mister Bronston if he's read the book, and he said yes. He told me the part about the one secret Japanese spy is true. I can't wait to buy the second Mickey Mathews novel, *The Long Pursuit*.

Late that afternoon, after taking a bath and changing clothes, I picked up Linda. We drove to the Lafayette Theater, and I parked in the lot for the 5:30 show of *This Gun for Hire*. We met Walt and Wanda near the ticket window, and by surprise, Herb and Iris also came. Herb told us he's wanted to see this movie for months, partly because it takes place in wartime San Francisco and stars big names like Veronica Lake, Robert Preston, and a new young actor, Alan Ladd.

We bought our tickets and went inside, taking six seats in a row by the rear wall. In no time the lights dimmed, and we watched the *MovieTone News* highlight how the British troopship *Erinpura* was sunk in the Mediterranean Sea by German bombers, an attack that killed over 800 British soldiers and sailors. It made me think about the cruelty of war.

But soon *This Gun for Hire* began. We watched as "hit man" Philip Raven, played by Alan Ladd, was hired by the bulky Willard Gates, played by Laird Cregar. Gates runs a business called Nitro Chemicals in Los Angeles, and he sends Raven after blackmailing chemist Baker, who stole a formula important to the US war effort. Raven kills Baker with a .45 pistol and recovers the formula, but he learns Gates double-crossed him by paying for the shooting with marked $10 bills. Still, the murder brings in LA Police Lieutenant Michael Crane, portrayed by the familiar Robert Preston. Crane is vacationing in San Francisco, and he leads the search for Raven.

Ellen Graham, played by the glamorous Veronica Lake, is the heroine. Miss Graham is hired as a singer at Gates' night club, but she fools him by meeting with a US senator and agreeing to spy on Gates and Nitro. While Gates and Baker are actually traitors to the war effort, Graham is the girlfriend of Crane, and she goes back and forth between the good guys and the bad guys.

The plot is twisted, but in the end the gunman, or Alan Ladd, makes Ellen help him escape. Later, Raven, the LA policeman, forces Gates, the businessman, to sign a confession, and the suspense builds. Raven is mortally wounded in a shootout with the police. As he lies dying, he casts loving eyes on Ellen, or Veronica Lake. She takes the confession, Raven dies, Crane arrives to kiss Graham, and seconds later we saw *The End*.

When the lights went up, Herb and Iris were kissing. Surprised for a moment, they smiled and stood up with the rest of us. They walked out of the aisle first, Linda and I came after them, and Walt and Wanda followed. In the lobby we passed a large crowd waiting for the 7:45 show. I told Linda what I thought about Raven, and, whispering, she said she admired Ladd's character. Outside on the sidewalk, Herb surprised me with his reaction,

"What the heck," he said. "I guess the movie bigwigs at a company like Paramount Pictures have to play it that way because of the Hays Code. The way my dad explained it, the code says that movies can't show a killer as a hero, or make him look sympathetic to the viewers. In the end, killers have to be punished for their crimes. So Alan Ladd's Raven, well, he's gotta die."

Not having heard of the Hays Code, I skipped that and suggested we all go to Sammy's. The idea turned everyone's attention to our date, and they agreed. The three guys drove in our cars with our dates, and in a few minutes we were sitting in a booth. Abraham, the waiter I saw before, appeared. Recognizing me, he grinned. "Why don't you and your lady friend order first?"

The courteous waiter jotted down my order of a hamburger with lettuce, tomato, and mayonnaise, Linda's request for a ham sandwich, and I ordered Coca-Colas for us. Iris asked for a grilled cheese sandwich and a Coke, and Herb wanted a hamburger with all the trimmings, French fries, and a strawberry shake. Walt and Wanda wanted a hamburger with everything as well as a Coca-Cola.

Abraham smiled, bowed, and left for the kitchen. Linda, watching him walk away, asked "Why do you suppose so many waiters and waitresses and cooks in diners and restaurants are Negroes, and always so polite? They *never* question what you say."

Iris looked at us. "Do you guys ever play any baseball teams with any Negro ballplayers?"

I shook my head. "Dad explained that to me a couple of years ago. He said the schools in this state, and the schools in many states, are segregated by law, which goes back to the *Plessy versus Ferguson* Supreme Court decision in the 1890s. The ruling legalized laws for racial segregation by upholding the principle of 'separate but equal.' Dad says we don't always see the *equal*, but in Virginia, it means athletic teams must be separated. He said: "It isn't fair, but it's the law.""

Wanda, leaning close to Walt, looked embarrassed. "I've heard my father and mother talking about those questions more than once. I gather Dad thinks it's a good idea. When I asked my mother about segregation, she said, 'Well, I wouldn't want to be segregated. Would *you*?'"

Iris, sitting across from Herb and beside Linda and me, was listening. She smiled sweetly. "Well, we all know about segregation, but you know, it's one of those sensitive issues that people don't like to talk about. The last time I heard my father mention it came when we moved here from Roanoke, and I was starting the ninth grade. I noticed that Jefferson High is all-white, and when I pointed that out to Mom, she said: 'The so-called Jim Crow laws don't bother me. I don't want Iris going to a school where you have to deal with all those 'race mixing' problems.'"

Abraham returned carrying four of our plates, one on each arm and hand. A dark-haired teenage girl in a white apron and cap followed him with the other two orders. Abraham set each plate in its proper place, bowed, and he and the waitress left. We started eating, and the subject of schools and teams didn't come up again. I was thinking ahead about having Linda in our Chevy on the way home, and what to do along the way.

Chapter 10

Girlfriends and the Cabin

A few minutes after we arrived home from church on Sunday, Aunt Cora made us a lunch of ham sandwiches, potato salad, and apple pie. After we ate, Nat and I went upstairs to do homework. Sitting at my desk, my eyes landed on my desk calendar: May 9. It reminded me that summer is coming. Since we had finished our American History textbook, Mister Bronston is digging up interesting information from magazines like *Time* and *Life* to tell us about the Allied forces fighting the German and Italian armies in places like Tunisia.

Looking over my notebook, my mind kept drifting back to yesterday's game, the triple date at the movies, and, afterward, the food and fun at Sammy's. Herb had Iris with him, Walt had Wanda, and again I took Linda. I know she likes going to the movies with me, because we kissed each other more than once during *This Gun for Hire*. My friends let on that they didn't see us smooching, but I saw them when they were kissing.

On Saturday evening after the six of us finished eating and emerged from Sammy's, I heard an angry yell from the parking lot beside the diner. Looking that way, I saw a Negro teenager close to my height being pushed around by three white teens. The black youth tried to walk away, but the tallest of the antagonists, with dark eyes, big shoulders, and a sneer on his tanned face, yelled, "What're you? A *chicken*!? Stand and fight, like a *man*!"

His buddy, a short guy with a dark crewcut and a leather jacket, moved up in the target's face, pointed up, and when the other teen's eyes followed, the bully knocked him down with a fist to the gut. Before the victim could catch his breath and scramble to his feet, the third attacker, a lean blonde-headed youth with a pug nose, kicked him.

Seeing the young man taking a beating, I turned to Herb and Walt, who were talking to their girls, and yelled, "There's a fight!"

I took off running, thinking *I gotta help him*. In a few seconds I reached the scene, but the bullies all turned on me. The tall guy with the dark eyes and big shoulders swung at me, but I ducked. He snarled, "Another *chicken*, huh? We're gonna fix you too, bud!"

The other two grabbed my arms from behind, and the first teen, giving me the evil eye, snarled, "This is where you learn to mind your own business, fool," and he socked me in the chest.

Wincing with the pain, I raised my right leg and thumped him in the chest while I was trying to twist out of the grip of his friends. Suddenly Herb appeared. Cussing the two holding me, he slugged the short teen in the nose, ducked his partner's punch, and decked the blonde guy with a roundhouse to the jaw.

A moment later Walt joined the fray, and surprising the tall bully, socked him in the stomach. When the big guy grunted and sucked air, Herb knocked him flat with an uppercut to the chin.

"James, you okay?" Herb yelled. "C'mon, let's give these idiots a *real thumping*!" Turning to Walt, he added, "Good job, man! I didn't realize you're a street fighter!"

Before we could do more damage, the three toughs turned, ran across the street, and headed down an alley. My adrenalin was still pumping, but all three of us grinned at each other. It was a moment snatched from time when you know your friends are there for you.

Herb grinned and like a boxer, he took a couple of steps, bobbed his head, and tossed a one-two punch at an invisible opponent. Turning to me, he pumped my arm. "You held your own against the odds, James. You're one *tough hombre*!"

Turning to Walt, Herb added, "In the next fight, I want *you* on my side!"

At that moment we all looked at the young Negro, who was struggling to get to his feet. I extended a hand and helped him, and Walt said, "Hey, we should have gotten here sooner."

Herb stepped forward and shook hands. "What's your name, friend?"

He looked at us like we were too good to be true. "I'm Danny Lincoln. My cousin Abraham works here at the diner. I came by to see him, and I guess those three guys figured I was out of place, or an easy target. Anyway, they picked a fight."

We became better acquainted in the next few minutes, and suddenly Abraham appeared from the side door of Sammy's. "What's going on out here?" He looked us over with suspicious eyes. "Danny, you need to avoid these kinds of bullies. They're just out to make trouble."

Danny replied, "Let's go inside, and I'll explain."

The two cousins smiled at us and went into Sammy's, and we returned to our girlfriends to explain why we helped another teen we didn't even know.

At that point in my Sunday afternoon thoughts, I slipped one of Cora's homemade bookmarks into my spiral notebook. Getting up, I moved over to the window and gazed down at our corn fields and apple orchards. *The day is bright and sunny*, I thought, *a cool breeze is making the weather pleasant, and I can see four robins flying back and forth in our yard.*

I couldn't seem to get much homework done. Maybe my thoughts about yesterday's fight with the three tough guys was stuck in my mind. I sat down on my bed, removed my shoes, and flopped on my back, resting my head on the pillow.

In no time my mind returned to yesterday's date, the fun at the movie, and talking with the girls at Sammy's about segregation. Afterward, I drove Linda back to her house, and my wrist watch showed the time was 8:35.

Darkness had descended, and that helped. I parked on the opposite side of the Lawtons' street, two houses past theirs. Linda had slipped over next to me. A streetlight stood about 20 yards in front of us, but the light left the Chevy's interior all but dark. Smiling, I faced her. "I hope you liked the movie."

She looked up at me with those big brown eyes, leaned closer, and we kissed. About 20 minutes later she said softly, "I want to see *Once Upon a Honeymoon*, with Cary Grant and Ginger Rogers … But James, movie talk can wait, *can't it*!"

We hugged and kissed again and again, and the time melted away. When I finally checked my watch, I couldn't believe it. "Linda, hang on. It's almost 10:00. I better take you inside."

She put her finger on my lips. "Why don't we just linger a while …?"

But we lingered, and the next time I looked, my watch said 10:15. I smiled at her. "I don't want to upset your mother, so let's agree we can see a movie whenever we like!"

Linda smoothed her hair, replaced the touch of lipstick she had when I picked her up, and we climbed out of the car. Holding hands, we walked along their sidewalk, climbed the steps, and the porch light blinked on. At the door, she looked up in my eyes. "Well, James, that's my mother saying it's *that time*." She kissed me on the cheek. "See you at school on Monday!"

She disappeared inside, and moments later the porch light went off. Floating back to the car, I started the engine and drove home carefully along the dark roads. Later, lying upstairs in my bed, I kept smiling about Linda. I thought, *Life is getting better. I love these movie dates and the time together with Linda … especially afterward.*

II

"James, are you awake?!"

Nat's voice startled me, and I sat up. "It's Sunday afternoon, remember? You look like you dozed off."

Perched in my captain's chair, she observed, "I want you to read my diary."

She held the blue-bound book out, I took it, and she grinned. "Saturday afternoon, after taking me to lunch, Ernie talked me into showing him the old cabin where Otto Herman and his Nazi sidekick Derek Miller stashed Karl Ellis and me last year, after they kidnapped us."

I grinned. "I'll read it, and I trust you. But how did Ernie know about Otto and the mountain cabin?"

"Well, I mentioned the experience earlier, and I guess I did mention the names, and, well, Ernie sounded interested, but we got to talking about it when we were leaving the restaurant."

I looked at her. "Nothing went wrong, I hope."

"Not really … but I want you to know what *did* happen." Nodding, she relaxed in the chair.

Opening the diary, I found a long entry about Saturday and started reading: *Ernie picked me up around noon in his Buick, and we drove to The Corner, where he parked at Sammy's. We found a booth, ordered sandwiches, Coca-Colas, and custard puddings, and we had a fun lunch.*

Afterward, when we went outside, he asked if we could drive up the mountain to the cabin where James and I had the confrontation with Otto Herman in the spring of 1942. At that point, Ernie, who's a handsome young man, came across as a nice guy. I thought he could be trusted, so I agreed.

He seemed gentle, especially after he told me how his 'birth father' abandoned him and his mother, Ann Brown, an English woman who was quite pretty and really nice. She told him his father emigrated to America sometime in the 1920s, and she thought he ended up in New York. It turns out that NYU gave Ernie the name of Karl Ellis as a student who could give him advice about colleges and college life. Karl even told him about UVA and about his experience with us last year. The result was that when Ernie got to Charlottesville, he already knew who I was.

I told Ernie I remembered the way to the cabin, and as it worked out, we spent over an hour on winding roads until we came to the country store, Elmer's Emporium. That's when Ernie noticed his gas was low, but he had two coupons and plenty of cash. We stopped, and he went inside and found Cecil, who was helping his dad at the cash register. Cecil came out, and said 'Hi!' He grinned at me, cranked up the pump, and put several gallons of gas into Ernie's car.

Smiling to myself, I kept reading: *I knew Cecil and my big brother had become friends, but I hadn't seen Cecil in a long time. Once he drove all the way to our house for dinner, but that's not all. I always had the impression that Cecil was 'stuck' on me, but I hoped he wouldn't ask me out. I would have turned him down. He's just not my type. I like guys who are a little different and exciting, like Ernie Herbert and Henry Wolinski, the senior who likes me.*

Cecil and I chatted after he finished pumping gas. I introduced him to Ernie, and Cecil didn't offer to shake hands. He's still the down-home country boy, clever, friendly, but maybe a little crooked. I told him about what my brother is doing, and he grinned. Fortunately, when he asked, I mentioned we were looking for the mountain cabin. Cecil told us how to get there.

He said the way had changed a little from last year, because for the past month a fallen tree has been blocking the road we used before. Anyhow, Cecil gave a complicated bunch of directions which Ernie seemed to understand. He paid up, and we took off again, only driving slower. In half an hour we found the mailbox and the trail back into the woods. Ernie turned off, drove through the trees, and suddenly there it was.

When I saw the cabin, all the memories came flooding back. I saw visions of Otto kidnapping Karl and me, bringing us there, and tying us up like animals. I couldn't forget that evil Derek putting his hands on me, even trying to get my blouse off, but thankfully Otto stopped him.

I watched Ernie knock on the door. The cabin has a forlorn look, like people have given it up. A line of black birds was perched on the peak of the roof, and the knocking scared them into flight. Nobody answered, Ernie tried the door, and it was unlocked. He beckoned to me. Taking a deep breath, I summoned the courage to leave the pickup.

I told Ernie to follow me, and we walked around in the back. I pointed out the slope leading down to the outhouse, and behind it where the yard drops off into the ravine. Seeing that once bloody spot in front of the outhouse, I started crying. I couldn't help myself.

Earlier Ernie appeared agitated, but now his demeanor turned patient and kind. 'You have come this far and now you are reliving the experience. You must tell me what happened that day.'

We went inside the cabin, and he had me sit in a chair at the table and give him an exact description of that day. He said I needed to relive what happened so I can move beyond it and turn the nightmare into ancient history. He said, 'This is psychodrama, a method of psychotherapy developed by a Romanian named Jacob Moreno around World War I.'

Ernie carries an elastic band in his pocket. From what he said, I think it came from the waist of his father's old pajamas, something his mother gave him. I guess he's attached to the band because it belonged to his father who he never knew. He likes curling it around a finger and stretching it to the elbow. When I first saw it, I called it his 'stretchy fidget.' He pulled that band from his pocket and asked me how my hands were tied that day. I said, 'In front of me.' He had me hold out my hands, and he wound the band tightly around my wrists.

I stopped reading and looked at my sister. "I don't get it. *What* was going on?"

"Well, Ernie said he wanted me to participate in this psychotherapy to get rid of my bad dream."

"Nat, doesn't a person doing this kind of thing have to be trained and licensed, not just an amateur?"

"Look, Big Brother, we were already in the cabin, and I thought he wanted to help …"

Shaking my head, I resumed reading: *Ernie asked me to show him how I picked up the fallen revolver. At first I didn't want to, but he insisted. Tears began rolling down my cheeks, and I leaned over and pretended to scoop up the gun James dropped. I gripped it between my two hands, and I pretended to stand over Otto, who sank to his knees after James shot him in the chest. Suddenly I saw a vision of Otto kneeling in front of me, and my brother lying there after having been shot. As I pretended to pull the trigger, I could almost hear the loud bangs.*

I looked up. "Nat, you should have quit at that point."

She nodded. "Actually, I wanted to stop, and in a few minutes Cecil showed up. You remember him, right?"

"Of course, his dad runs Elmer's Emporium, that country store on the mountain. A little earlier in the diary you wrote about stopping there."

I took a deep breath and continued reading: *I sank to my knees, and from behind me, Ernie lifted me up by my shoulders. I felt dazed and sad, and my heart seemed ready to burst. He was standing behind me with his hands gently around my neck. He put his mouth close to my ear and whispered, 'I am going to tell you a secret.'*

At that moment, we heard knocking on the door. Before we could move, the door swung open and there stood Cecil from the store. He had the butt of a revolver sticking out of his pants pocket, and I'm pretty sure it was the gun Dad gave him for helping us last year.

Cecil took a couple of steps toward us, he said, 'What's going on here?'

I managed to smile, and I told Cecil everything was fine. He gave me a questioning look, and he said, 'I got to worryin' about whether you folks might have got yourselves lost. I was watchin' for you to pass the store on the way home, and I never saw the Buick, so I came lookin' for you.' Taking a closer look, Cecil saw my tear-stained face, and his hand dropped to the gun butt.

Behind me, Ernie's hands left my neck, and he muttered 'Mein Gott.' I never heard him speak German before, and I wondered why an Englishman would speak German.

'Are you really okay?' Cecil stared at me. I waved my hand at the back yard outside, and said, 'Out there is where it all happened. I had a bad moment with the old memories, but it's over.'

Ernie chimed in, saying, 'We are playing a little psychotherapy game, and Natalia will not again have any bad memories.' He smiled, but out of the corner of my eye I could see beads of sweat on his forehead. He just couldn't take his eyes off that gun.

Cecil looked doubtful, but he's clever. He told us about a storm brewing, and we needed to get off the mountain as soon as possible. 'I can see some of these ol' old pine trees fallin' here in the woods. It plain ain't safe.'

Ernie realized Cecil wasn't leaving, so we went outside. He thanked Cecil for telling us about the storm, and sure enough, we saw the dark clouds whirling above. We said goodbye, and Cecil still had his hand on the gun butt.

Once we got in the car and Ernie drove back onto the narrow road, he asked if I was giving back his 'stretchy fidget.' I pulled it off my wrist and flipped it in his lap. I said, 'You don't want to tie me up again, do you?' Ernie looked surprised, but he kept driving.

I said, 'So what was the big secret that you were going to tell me when Cecil popped up?' He just laughed and said honestly he couldn't remember. The rest of the drive we talked about Charlottesville, and college, and apartments, but we didn't say any more about the cabin and what happened. He dropped me off at home an hour and a half later, and he left.

I closed her diary, looked at her, and handed it back. "I'm glad you let me read about your afternoon, Sis, but I'm wondering about Ernie, and his motives, and his goals."

"I think he just wanted to help me, so I don't want to jump to any false conclusions. Other than making me do this psychotherapy thing, Ernie couldn't have been more of a gentleman."

Flashing a smile, Nat returned to her bedroom. I could tell she didn't want to say any more. Closing the door, I flopped on the bed on my back. Staring at the light globe, I reflected on the new cabin episode. The more I thought, the more I relaxed. Before long I climbed up to a low fluffy cloud and floated away. The clouds around me were carried by the wind toward Afton Mountain. I looked down and saw the peaks, and we passed over into the Shenandoah Valley. After a while,

I think I saw the distant Ohio River as it curved south away from Pittsburgh.

A soft voice started speaking close to me. "James, wake up." Someone was shaking my arm. "I have some questions about my English paper."

I opened my eyes, and Nat smiled at me. "Sorry, Big Brother, you looked so peaceful. But it's close to 4:30, and I need to finish this essay."

Sitting up, I looked around, but the Ohio River had vanished. I stood up, ran a hand through my hair, and walked down the hall to her room to look over the essay.

Chapter 11

Last Week of School

On Monday morning at breakfast, everyone seemed in a good mood. Aunt Cora had cooked pancakes, eggs, and sausage, and made coffee. Dad, who started his work at sunrise, walked inside and called it a beautiful day. Taking the cue, Nat told us about the activities she anticipated in our last week of school.

I smiled. "Our guys are hoping for an unbeaten season as we get ready for the final baseball game of 1943. The war and rationing stuff like gasoline made it so we can't play as many games this year, but we can't do anything about that."

After breakfast Nat came along and I drove the pickup to school. On the way she said Aunt Cora revealed to her that she and Dad spent some pleasant time together last night. Life seems to be going well on the Baker farm, but I wondered: What about Nat and her boyfriend Ernie? What about Dad and Helen LaSalle?

Still, school ends this week, and you can tell because the teachers are easing up. Everyone knows summer is around the corner. For me, summer is the best time of the year. The weather is warmer, we play baseball with the Broncos in the summer league, and I have a girlfriend I'm going to ask to go steady. In the summer the farm work is mostly maintenance jobs, because the plowing and planting are done. And the harvest, the real busy time of the year, is more than three months away.

Later, sitting in Mister Bronston's American History class, my mind wandered to Ernie. What is he *really* like? But a strong voice interrupted my thoughts. "*Wake up*, Mister Baker. Give us your thoughts on how the world war is going for America in 1943."

Mister Bronston caught me off guard, but I rebounded nicely. "Actually, I have been thinking about that. I believe our armed forces will be really strong when they team up with the Allies, and sooner or later, they will invade Europe. I think the Allies will figure out the place they can invade where the Nazi Germans and the fascist Italians will least expect it. I don't know where, but I'll bet President Roosevelt and Prime Minister Churchill are talking about it."

Mister Bronston nodded, and looking thoughtful, he steered the discussion back to the Home Front. Most of my classes went along similar lines. At home Dad often talks about the war. He thinks the American people will trust President Roosevelt to do the right thing, and I hope he's right. Still, the US has a long way to go in order to win the Second World War.

That evening we enjoyed dinner at 6:00, a pot roast along with cooked carrots and mashed potatoes. That meal tasted like a feast for a king and his family. Aunt

Cora really can cook, and afterward, Dad said, "Cora, you are one of the *best* cooks I've ever known. Despite the rationing and the coupons and all, you keep coming up with these swell meals!"

Nat made a real nice comment too, and I agreed. Even as we complimented Aunt Cora, I was thinking about visiting Missus LaSalle and telling her what I learned in Roanoke. When the dishes were done, Dad and Aunt Cora walked into the living room to relax. Nat said she had homework to do, and she went upstairs. By then I had invented a "cover story."

Finding Dad in the living room, I said, "I might have left my baseball spikes in the locker room. We practiced today, and I want to be ready for tomorrow's game with Blue Ridge."

Looking up at me, Dad smiled. "Well, take the pickup and drive to the high school. Do you think a janitor will be around to let you in the locker room?"

"Yeah, I'm pretty sure someone works until 11:00. Mister Blackburn is one janitor, and the other is Mister Davis. I've heard they rotate between the early and late shifts."

Walking out the back door about 7:15, I thought, *That's the first time I deliberately lied to Dad.* Steeling myself, I climbed in the pickup, started the engine, and drove toward town. I was thinking about what to say, but I concluded the right words would come. Twenty minutes later, I parked across from the LaSalle house on Fifth Street, a couple of blocks north of Main.

Getting out of the pickup, I looked at the two-story white house with its gables, blue roof, wide front porch, and lights shining in several windows downstairs and one window upstairs. Downstairs the windows had the curtains closed, and upstairs shades were pulled. Walking up on the porch and crossing it, I knocked on the door. After a short wait, the door opened on a chain, and Missus LaSalle peeked out. She looked surprised, but recognizing me, she opened the door.

"Hi, James." Her voice sounded melodious, almost like Ingrid Bergman. "How are you?"

She gave me a curious look with her wide blue eyes. Looking at her, you couldn't miss her natural beauty. She had high cheeks in her ivory face, dark eye shadow under her eyes, and maroon lipstick freshly applied. She smiled sweetly, almost like she was flirting.

"Come in and sit down. Would you like a drink, or a glass of iced tea, or something?"

Shaking my head no, I walked in and looked around. The large room looked was furnished with red carpet, a maroon mohair couch, two matching easy chairs, three bronze floor lamps with maroon shades, and a dark bookcase filled with books. Three doors led to other rooms.

I sat down slowly on the couch. Sitting in an easy chair opposite me, she crossed her legs. I wondered if she was planning to go somewhere, because she was wearing a low-necked blue blouse, a black skirt, and black high heels.

Nodding, I forged ahead. "I need to talk to you, and I'm sorry if it's late."

As I started to speak, I noticed two wine glasses sitting on the end table to my right, and one had dark red smudges. Ignoring the glasses, I focused on her. "Several days ago I drove to Roanoke to use the local library downtown …"

Raising her eyebrows, she cut me off: "Were you doing research for one of those high school term papers? I always hated doing those." Suddenly her smile seemed strained.

"Actually, I wondered about your background. My sister Natalia and I understand you used to be a church secretary in Roanoke. That must have been a lot like your position in our church."

She frowned. "You wondered about *my* background?" Her eyes turned cold. "I have told your father all about my background … he trusts me, I'm proud to say."

I expected that. "Yes, well, I got to digging into the old yearbooks and newspapers at the Roanoke library, and I found some different information. Monroe High's 1926 yearbook shows that Helen LaSalle, a senior, passed away earlier in the year. The yearbook has a black ribbon around her senior picture. So I looked at all the pictures of girls graduating from Monroe in 1926, and I saw your picture over the name *Abigail Evans*."

She gasped, and her face turned pale, but I kept going. "When I looked up Abigail Evans in the card catalog, I found a note saying to check on Abigail *Shaw*. When I looked in the Shaw folder, I found a clipping indicating Abigail Shaw was convicted and sent to prison for three years for embezzling $5,000 from a church where she worked as secretary."

Feeling relieved that I managed to get out my planned comments, I watched as she replied, her voice barely above a whisper. "What are you going to do with that … *awful information?*"

Searching for the best words, I said, "Since you and Dad are getting serious in your courtship, I think he should know more about your background in Roanoke."

The living room fell so silent I could hear her breathing. "In fact," I added, "I think *you* should be the one to tell him."

After a pause, she gave me another smile. "Look, James. I don't think your father, or anyone else, needs to know what I suffered through in Roanoke during those years. After all, I've served my sentence, and I'm a changed woman. If it hadn't been for my husband abandoning me and Joyce, I wouldn't have needed the money."

She paused, and I felt her eyes drilling into mine, but I wasn't intimidated. "Here is what I've decided. I'll give you until Saturday to tell Dad about this. You can pick the time, but it has to be *this week*. Otherwise, I'll have to show him the notes I took in Roanoke. I have the name of the librarian, and the library's phone number, in case he wants to verify anything."

Helen, or Abigail, broke into tears, and she sobbed for several minutes. Finally, looking at me through teary eyes, she sat up straight. "I'm not sure whether trying to help raise a stepson and stepdaughter who would betray me and my Joyce would be worth the time and effort."

Standing up, she glared at me. "I've heard enough."

I got to my feet, watching her. She walked briskly to the front door, pulled it open, and said quietly, "Goodbye, and *good riddance*."

I walked out, across the porch, and to the sidewalk in front, where I encountered an elderly gentleman gripping the leash to a little white poodle with a red ribbon tied around its neck. Seeing me, he raised his derby hat, smiled, and said, "Good evening, young man!"

Wishing him a good evening, I crossed the street and got into the truck. Starting the engine, I turned and looked at her house. Sighing, I felt like a heavy burden had been lifted from my shoulders. The front door was closed, but the same lights were on. I saw two figures silhouetted on the living room curtains near the lamps. I realized she had a visitor, but I didn't care.

Accelerating, I drove out of town and back to our farm. On the way I concentrated on my driving, but there was virtually no traffic. After parking, I climbed out and stood in the darkness. Overhead I saw the black carpet of the sky dotted with stars sparkling like one of nature's wonders. I didn't feel good about what I had to tell Missus Shaw, but I'm sure Dad would feel betrayed if he uncovered her hidden background. So I just walked into our home.

II

On Tuesday afternoon our players hurried to the locker room after Jefferson High's 2:00 bell rang. Coach Jackson greeted everyone at the door, saying we needed to change in a hurry. Coach Spencer stood outside the office, watching as we pulled on our uniforms and put gloves, cleats, and other gear in our duffel bags. When Ray Riley opened the locker room door, he was told to pull the bus as close to the school as possible. Fifteen minutes later, Coach Spencer talked to us on the side bench.

"This will be our last varsity game of 1943," he said quietly, "and as you know, we're traveling to Harrisonburg to play a larger school, Blue Ridge High. We've never played them before, but I expect a real tough game." He looked at all of us. "Still, I hope we will be able to play everyone today. And remember, if we can win, it means an *undefeated* season for Jefferson."

That was it. The coach waved toward the parking lot, and Coach Jackson held the locker room door open. We got up from the bench and walked gingerly across the floor. Jackson had an encouraging word or two for each of us as we passed him.

Several minutes later, Mister Riley turned the bus north on US-29. The trip would take more than an hour, but nobody cared. As usual, you could hear quiet remarks as guys talked to their seat partner or with another teammate across the aisle. At first you're aware of the shifting of gears and the rumbling of the engine on a bus trip, but before long it becomes background noise.

The day was warm, maybe in the lower 70s, but dark clouds filled the sky. In a few minutes a bolt of lightning zigzagged down into a tree alongside the highway. The flash of light preceded by moments a rolling *boom* of thunder that startled most of us. As Mister Riley turned west on US-33 to cross the mountain, the sky opened and rain pounded down for five or six minutes.

When the sun finally broke through, the dark clouds vanished like giant hands had swept them away. After another half hour, the bus pulled into the Blue Ridge parking lot. Grabbing our duffel bags and bats, we clambered off the bus and followed Coaches Spencer and Jackson to the baseball field behind the school. The diamond had a standard setup with wooden benches on each side, chain link fences all around, and a chain link backstop with boards or a metal panel about 7-8 feet high placed in the middle. The crowd almost filled the home team's third base side of the bleachers, but maybe three dozen spectators were sitting on the first base side.

We headed to the bench for instructions. Once we were seated, Coach Spencer looked us over. "We're gonna start Matt Richards today at pitcher. We've had a good season, and maybe we'll have a little fun today!"

Spencer smiled, and Coach Jackson took his turn. "We may try a new pitcher or two today, so it's gonna be a real *team effort*!"

By that time Matt, who had grown to almost six feet tall and filled out over the winter, was throwing warmups to Herb Jenkowski behind the bench. In a minute or two, Herb stood up hustled over to Matt. "You have to be ready. We bat first, and I might get up to bat."

Looking nervous, Matt just nodded. A junior like many of us, he had short brown hair, big brown eyes, and a medium frame. Nat likes him, and she told me that Matt earns A's in all his classes. But in baseball this spring, he's pitched in only one game, and he didn't seem confident that day.

Leading off for Jefferson, Jack Jones stepped in, took a couple of his left-handed swings, and stared at the pitcher, Peter Purcell, a tenth grader. On the first pitch, Jack turned a fastball into a booming triple to straight away center field that rattled off the fence. Next came Scott, batting second, and Purcell pitched from the stretch. He started with a good curve, but Scott doubled to left center, allowing Jack to score. Hitting in the third slot, I ripped the first pitch for a single over third base, scoring Matthews. Up came Herb in the cleanup slot, and he was swishing his big bat. On the second pitch, he slammed a home run over a 300-foot sign on the left field fence. When he trotted around and stepped on home plate, just after I did, he gave us a big smile. Jefferson led, 4-0.

Blue Ridge Coach Mickey Hamilton, who Coach Spencer said he knows, is a young dark-haired Social Studies teacher who likes coaching too. From the bench, Hamilton sent out a new pitcher, Gary Rolfe, a junior right-hander. But Rolfe didn't have good control, and his teammates finally recorded the third out after we built a 7-0 lead.

Our guys were feeling pretty good, until Matt gave up a double to their first batter. The next two hitters drew bases on balls, and three straight guys singled. Coach Spencer came out to settle Matt down, but he still looked shaky. Finally, he got some fastballs and sidearm curves over the plate, and the fielders bailed us out, making three good catches. We led after the first inning, but only 7-6.

In the top of the second, Coach Hamilton put in Stan Skucovich to pitch. Skucovich was a six-one crewcut tenth grader that his teammates didn't look happy to see. We managed to work his jerky pitching style for three hits, one walk, and one run in each of his two innings.

Coach Spencer switched Matt to second base, and he moved Andy Thornton to pitcher. Despite lacking pitching experience or a good curveball, Andy just kept throwing hard. He gave up three runs on four hits and two bases on balls in two innings. By then Blue Ridge had tied us, 9-9.

In the top of the fourth, I was talking quietly with Herb. He muttered something about "our crazy pitching." Sitting on the other side of Herb, Jack murmured something quite critical. Like the other regulars, I wondered what was happening. Blue Ridge's coach subbed Graham Redstone, a rangy sophomore left-hander, and he pitched two shaky innings. We racked up two runs each in the fourth and fifth inning, and most of us hoped we were on the road to victory.

In the last of the fourth, Coach Spencer shifted Damon Vann from shortstop to pitcher, and he moved Andy to short. Damon pitched two innings, but his curve wasn't breaking well. He kept throwing what Herb called for, but the home team collected four runs, six hits, and two walks. When the dust settled after the fifth inning, Blue Ridge had tied Jefferson once again, 13-13.

The high score bothered me. When I whispered to Jack about all the pitching substitutions, he remarked, "It's like Spencer's tryin' to *give* the game away."

In the top of the sixth Coach Hamilton sent in a stocky-right handed junior, Bob Anderson. He had good speed, but I connected with a good fastball and doubled to right center. Before our at-bats ended, Jefferson scored three times for a 16-13 lead. The see-saw game continued in the bottom of the sixth when Coach Spencer called on Walt Bunker to pitch. Walt didn't fool many batters with his curveballs, and with two outs, Blue Ridge had scored three times to knot the score at 16-16.

Looking over at the coaches with a Blue Ridge runner at third, Herb called time. Waving, he trotted out to talk to Walt. Herb got in his face, but Walt kept looking down. Herb, keeping his back to home plate, signaled to me, Damon, and Andy, and we hurried over. The infield umpire, a tall man with the usual blue shirt and gray slacks, was standing in front of second base. He gave me a stern look as I put my head in the huddle.

Herb ran his gaze over us. "Get ready. Any hit scores the runner, and then we're behind, 17-16. Walt, throw your best hard curve." As Walt nodded vigorously, Herb looked at the three of us. "If the batter hits a grounder, you gotta field that ball and *throw him out*! We gotta save *the tie*!"

We all nodded, and Herb grinned. "*Let's go!*"

We returned to our position, Walt got ready to pitch, and the umpire yelled "*Play ball!*"

Taking his stretch, Walt checked the runner at third, and he threw his best curve of the day. Billy Twoshoes, their speedy shortstop, bounced a grounder past Walt. Damon raced in, grabbed the ball bare-handed, and flipped me a throw that bounced in the dirt to my left. Twoshoes all but flew down the baseline, and at the last second he leaped for the base, extending his right foot.

Ready, I stretched to my right and made a back-handed scoop, and I heard the runner's spikes hit the bag just after I felt the ball hit my glove's webbing. The umpire, Mister Barlick, the Blue Ridge principal, hesitated. He took a close look at me with one foot on the base, the other foot extended, and the ball in my trapper's mitt, and yelled "You are *outta there!*"

There was no time to talk about the fine plays we made for the third out. The score was tied, and we needed to score in the top of the seventh inning. Bob James, batting in the ninth slot, led off. On Anderson's second fastball, Bob looped a single to left field. Jack batted next. After digging in with his cleats and swishing his bat, he smashed a line drive just over the first baseman's mitt for a double, sending Bob speeding around to third. Scott stepped in, studied the pitcher, took two balls and a strike, and he popped up a curveball, and the first baseman snagged it for one out.

Batting next, I felt nervous. Getting into my stance, I took a couple of practice swings. Bob took a big lead from third base. Anderson, taking his stretch, fooled me on a curveball, and I topped one back to the pitcher. He fielded it to his left, turned, and threw to home plate, but Bob took off the second I swung the bat, and he slid under the catcher's tag. The umpire, on top of the play, spread his arms wide to signal safe!

Jefferson had a 17-16 lead! When their catcher looked around, Jack had reached third base on the throw home and I was standing on first.

Herb batted next with a chance to boost our lead, and he *really* came through. Anderson uncorked a dinky slider, and Herb lined a low single to right center. Their right fielder came rushing in, fielded the ball on one hop, and threw a strike to home plate, but Jack scored easily. Now we led by two runs, 18-16, and I ended up at third base while Herb held at first.

Walt batted next, and I crossed my fingers. Fooled by a curveball, he grounded to the shortstop, who started a double play, short to second to first! It marked the only time Jefferson hit into a double play in the 1943 season.

Following our at-bats, I saw Herb talking to Coach Spencer. As we grabbed our gloves and started to take the field, the coach waved everyone to the bench. "Okay, I'm gonna say this since Herb asked, and Jack wants to know too. Maybe you *all* want to know."

He kicked the dirt. "I started out to play everyone today, and try some new pitchers, so … maybe I went too far. But *nobody* can say we didn't come here to win. I know Bob is ready, and he's gonna pitch the seventh. The rest of you, get out there and play baseball like the fine ballplayers you are!"

Coach Jackson stood beside Spencer, and he looked us over. "You guys might think coach and I don't compare notes, but we do. I heard the rumbles on the bench, but we've got an ace too. So we want you out there giving your best. Now, go show these guys how *tough* you play ball!"

As we took the field, our chances looked good. Bob took his warmups, I lobbed bouncers to the infielders, and soon we were ready and anxious to go. The home crowd was chanting "Go, *Blue Ridge*! GO, *Blue Ridge*!"

Terry Gordon, their senior third baseman, took two strikes and one ball, and Bob almost had him on an outside curve, but he popped it into short right field for a single. Warren Johnson, the stubby catcher, singled to center, and that put runners on first and second base with nobody out. Pitching from the stretch, Bob suckered Tommy Tomkins, a stocky outfielder, with four straight curves, and Tomkins struck out swinging. One out, and we still led by two runs. Bob Anderson, the pitcher, was also a good hitter. He connected with a fastball and lined it into left center.

Both of their runners took off at the crack of the bat, and as they rounded third, Jones, playing left field, gloved the ball and cut loose a spectacular throw to home plate. Gordon, the first runner, scored standing up, but Johnson, the second guy and another senior, came sliding hard with his spikes high. Unfazed, Herb blocked the plate, tagging him hard on the foot.

Mister Barlick, the umpire, raised his right hand, signaling for the second out. Seeing Anderson trying to make it all the way to third base, Herb grabbed the ball from his mitt and fired a bullet to Scott at third. Scott, backhanding the throw inches above the ground, stepped aside and shoved the gloved ball in front of the sliding Anderson's spikes.

The infield umpire, watching from a few feet away, raised his right hand and declared, "You are *out*, and that is the *ball game*!"

Jefferson, with some fine fielding and throwing, had snatched victory from the jaws of defeat. But nobody wanted to hang around and celebrate. We hurried over and congratulated their guys, gathered up our equipment, and followed Coach Jackson onto the bus. Blue Ridge students and teachers were leaving through the same gate, and many were complaining about the "lousy umpiring."

Coach Spencer spent a few minutes talking with Coach Hamilton, and from a distance, they looked like good friends. Five minutes later, Spencer climbed on the bus. "Well, well, well," he said, a huge grin on his grizzled features. "Here you guys are wondering *what* was up with me!"

He waved off a question. "Their coach for today is Mickey Hamilton. He's a gym teacher and the nephew of my wife Adell. It seems the regular coach didn't record some players' grades correctly in a certain class, and the principal suspended the coach and four seniors for this game. To help his school, Mickey went out and gave it his best shot. I told him '*Way to go, coach!*'"

He turned to Ray Riley. "Let's get going, Ray." As the engine started and the bus rumbled toward the street, Coach Spencer smiled. "All of you are invited to our house on Friday afternoon for a picnic at 5:00. You can invite your parents, your girlfriends, or your friends, but just try to make it. Even though wartime rationing forced us to play fewer games, this has been a most rewarding season. I'd love to have you all back next year!"

Mister Riley turned the bus east onto US-33, and Coach Spencer added: "You guys go home tonight, finish this week of school, get your grades, and join us for the picnic!"

Chapter 12

Surprise, Ernie, and Summer

Wednesday was another easy day of classes. Everyone realizes the school year is virtually over, and the teachers aren't handing out homework. After classes ended at 3:00, I joined the other guys heading to the locker room to turn in our Jefferson uniforms. Aunt Cora had washed my jersey and pants and folded the uniform neatly, and I'm sure my friends had their mothers do the same. Of course, we keep the white cotton baseball undershirt with the long blue sleeves.

With the season over, the final day is bittersweet, but we did have a memorable year. Everyone was hanging around and talking with Coach Spencer and Coach Jackson about the undefeated season. In fact, a few teachers joined us to share in the fun. I think Mister Bronston, who umpires our home games, talked to everyone. In his World History and American History classes he's the stern taskmaster, but on the diamond, he loves baseball. We heard he's a Senators fan.

Today several other teachers went around shaking everyone's hand, offering praise, and laughing and joking. Mister Knudson, who teaches Geography and History, Mister Shears, who teaches Government classes, Mister Stevens, the counselor, and Miss Martin and Miss DeRoche all came to the locker room.

We heard Miss Martin saw a couple of games, and she was all smiles as she shook each player's hand. Miss DeRoche said she used to play softball in high school when she lived in Flint, Michigan. She told some funny stories about what she and her friends did in high school. As for me, it felt really cool to get to know some of our teachers as regular people.

Afterward, Herb, driving his father's black Ford, followed me in the pickup to our house. We arrived about 4:15. We wanted to talk about Coach Spencer and the Friday afternoon picnic. Seeing Dad had parked our tractor at the end of the driveway, Herb followed me, and we drove around behind the barn, where both of us parked.

We headed across the yard, entered the back door, and in the kitchen we greeted Dad and Aunt Cora, who were sitting across from each other at the table. They were enjoying lemonade, and Aunt Cora offered us a glass, too, but Herb politely declined. I indicated we had baseball stuff to talk about, and nodding, Dad smiled.

We went upstairs to my room, and I closed the door. Herb spotted my baseball bats and southpaw gloves. Picking up my trapper's mitt, he grinned. "You know what? We had great hitting, but all the good fielding we've had, well, it's our *gloves* that really saved the unbeaten season!"

He handed back the glove, and I smiled. "Yeah, well, I think the tough guy who's doing our catching probably saved all of our *pitchers*!"

Herb blushed slightly. "Thanks, buddy," and he gave me a huge smile. "But here's what I came to say. On Friday at Spencer's place, you should make a little speech about the coaches, and the players, and the season. You're a bright guy, and a good ballplayer, and I trust you to give a good talk, you know, *thanking* the coaches and all."

Caught by surprise, I smiled as the idea grew on me. "Yeah, *maybe* I can say some good words."

At that moment we heard a car pull into the driveway and brake. Two doors opened and closed, and a minute later, Nat's voice, unusually loud, could be heard from the kitchen: "I'm home, Dad and Aunt Cora. I have someone for you to meet!"

I opened my door, and we could hear voices better. I faced Herb. "I think Nat has that guy Ernie with her, and it sounds like she brought him here, well, to meet the family. Did I tell you about him?"

Herb studied me. "Is he the older guy you mentioned one time? He's an Englishman, right?"

He looked thoughtful. "What happened to Henry Wolinski? I thought Nat liked him."

Another vehicle, this one with a souped-up engine, pulled into the driveway, and we could hear the brakes on the gravel. The engine died, and we heard doors opening and shutting. Looking at each other, we didn't hear much for a few seconds.

Herb looked at me. "It's Wednesday afternoon. You expecting somebody else?"

When I shook my head no, he nodded toward the doorway. I opened the door a little so we could listen. A few seconds later we heard a harsh voice say: "Get inside there, you two. I mean *now!*"

Holding a finger to his lips, Herb slipped over beside me, and we both listened. The abrasive voice growled, "All right, buddy boy! You and your sister, you move over there against the back wall, by the phone!"

A pause followed. "And you, *old man* Baker. You and that woman of yours, you move over to the wall, beside the fridge. *Hear me*?!"

"Yes," came Dad's calm reply. "We hear, all right. But what do you two want?"

"This is a *hold-up*! You're gonna cough up yer cash, and yer war bonds, and you, woman ..." We heard a sharp *slap*, and Aunt Cora's cry of fear.

The deadly voice continued: "Now, buddy boy, your sister and you, you're gonna pull out your wallets, purses, whatever … or you're both gonna take a whack, like I gave the woman, *see*?!"

Next we heard the unpleasant *thump* of a fist on flesh. "Blimey!" Ernie wailed. "I didn't do anything! Besides, you think I'm *James*, her brother, but really, *I'm not!*"

I whispered to Herb: "Dad and Cora, they know you and I are up here, and probably so do Nat and Ernie."

He whispered: "*Listen!*"

"… my purse is upstairs, mister," Nat said, speaking in a high voice. "I can run upstairs and get it from my room … I went to the bank today for Dad … I've got *plenty of money!*"

We looked at each other, and I whispered: "My sister's trying to *set him up!*"

Herb nodded. "Yeah, she's clever!" He grinned wickedly. "We're gonna take these guys out, see, but *one at a time!*"

From below we heard a scratchy voice muttering, "You keep dem covered, and I'll take da girl upstairs, and grab da money … we ain't got much time, ya know."

After a pause the deadly voice replied, "But remember, it's *payback time!* This is the family that killed Otto Herman … God, I *loved* that man!"

"Get ready," Herb whispered. "When Nat and the gunman come up here, we've gotta take him out, but *quietly.*"

Closing my eyes, I said a quick prayer. Afterward, both of us peeked around the edge of the doorway. We heard Nat and her captor climbing the stairs. Reaching the landing, they walked past my room. I took two quick strides and touched his shoulder. A bulky six-footer, he spun around, his black eyes showing surprise, his curly brown hair out of sorts, and his jaw open.

Instinctively he raised his pistol to fire, but I swung my left, hitting him hard in the side of the jaw. The impact twisted his face into a contorted expression, and his dark eyes rolled up, but Herb moved past me and smashed his right fist into the thug's forehead.

Next to him, Nat stared, her greenish eyes opened wide. She watched in awe as we carefully lowered the unconscious thug onto the carpet. Turning to Nat, Herb motioned her over.

"Listen," he said quietly. "Get your purse, and try to act natural. James and me, we're gonna slip downstairs and hide next to the kitchen door."

When Nat's eyes flashed agreement, I thought *Herb called another pitch, and we have to make this into the game-winner*. Hurrying to her room, she returned in a few seconds with her blue strap bag looped over the right shoulder.

Nat came close to me and whispered: "What do I do?"

Already Herb had descended the stairs, and he flattened his back to the wall on the right side of the kitchen entrance. Pointing to him, I whispered: "Go back down to the kitchen and tell the other guy his buddy is up here, rummaging through your personal stuff. Act *outraged*!"

Again her eyes flashed. She went quietly down the stairs with me following, and in the dining room I slipped over behind Herb as Nat walked slowly into the kitchen. Herb's eyes signaled to do it as she strolled in the kitchen. The thug's low voice croaked *"Where's Clyde?"*

Nat, in emotional tones, declared, "He's up there rummaging through my dresser to find out what I *wear*. What kind of *creep* is he?!"

I heard footsteps, and the stubby, unshaven gunman holding a .45 semi-automatic pistol, poked his head through the door to look up to the second floor. He saw us, and started to raise his weapon, but Herb grabbed his right hand with his wrist, twisted the wrist, and with the other fist, hit him hard in the nose.

We heard an "*Arrgghh,*" as the intruder dropped his weapon and grabbed his bloody nose. He backed up a step, and groaned but Herb gave him a one-two punch like an angry boxer going for the knockout. The robber toppled backward onto the kitchen floor, and in a flash Herb jumped him. Rolling him over, Herb held his large arms behind his back.

I took a quick look around the kitchen. Ernie was holding onto Aunt Cora's arm, and both were backed up against the counter. Dad was retrieving the Colt revolver from the drawer where he stashed it. In front of me, Herb was on top of the robber, grinning. Lying face down, the grizzled gunman was mumbling in German.

Leaning down, I scooped up the gun. In moments Dad was standing over the robber, keeping him covered with the Colt .38. He looked at me. "*Where's* the other guy?"

"He's upstairs, Mister Baker," Herb replied, looking up at Dad. "He's in *dreamland*!"

For a moment Dad looked surprised, but he turned to me. "Let's go and make sure!"

Leaving Herb in charge and Aunt Cora and Ernie staring at the scene, I flew up the stairs with my father behind me. We found the first thug lying face down near the landing, breathing heavily. Dad turned to me.

"Get your baseball bat and guard him. I'm calling the sheriff! If he tries to get up, belt him!"

Dad descended the stairs two steps at a time, rushed into the kitchen, and dialed the wall phone. I heard him say: "Operator! Give me the Sheriff's Office! We have two thieves in our house, and they tried to rob us!" He recited the address.

Moments after Dad replaced the receiver, I heard Herb. "Mister Baker! I think there's a third crook outside in the car, in the driveway!"

Understanding, Dad, followed by Ernie, moved through the house into the living room. Later I learned he peeked around the curtains on the right front window. Turning to the others, he said something, but all I heard was "... doesn't seem to know anything went wrong in here with his partners."

As the clock in the hallway ticked, the guy I was guarding started to moan. When he turned over and looked up at me, I raised the bat. "We've called the sheriff, mister. If you get up before they come, I'm gonna *club you*."

I kicked him once in the side, and he yelped. "Do you understand?"

He nodded, turned his face down, and muttered something like "Verflixt." At that moment I heard a distant siren, and I thought *The sheriff and his deputies are on the way*!

We heard the sound of a car's engine starting in our driveway. When it did, I heard Dad open the front door, step outside, and yell: "*Stop, or I'll shoot!*"

Next I heard an engine accelerating, and moment later a loud *bang*! Brakes squeaked, and I heard nothing for maybe half a minute. Then came the sound of a car with a loud engine pulling into our driveway and jamming on the brakes. Doors opened and slammed closed, and I heard loud voices, followed by Dad yelling: "In *here*!"

In a few seconds I heard a gruff voice from the living room. "Zeke, *how* did you and your family do this? Do you have any idea who these thugs are?"

Dad replied, but I didn't pay attention to what he said because a tall, gray-uniformed deputy in a wide-brimmed hat was ascending the stairs, two steps at a time. He reached the landing, and I saw the tall man looking down at me and my captive, holding his weapon in both hands.

"Hey, young fella," he said, with a drawl. "My name's Charlie Powell. I'm a deputy sheriff. We've got this situation under control, but you and your friends downstairs, you all have done a great job!"

Taking handcuffs from his belt, Deputy Powell cuffed the thug's hands behind his back. Backing up, his brown eyes smiled as he yanked the guy to his feet. Watching, I breathed a sigh of relief. Little did I know, but Herb and I would soon be the talk of Jefferson High! Nor did I realize the local newspaper would describe Herb and me and Nat and Dad like folk heroes!

I followed the deputy and his prisoner downstairs, and I found Herb smiling and looking relieved. Twenty minutes later, once the deputies departed, Dad shook hands profusely with Herb and with me, and Aunt Cora and Nat embraced each other warmly. Ernie wanted to hug Nat, but she kept holding hands with Aunt Cora. As it turned out, Ernie didn't hang around long, but before leaving, he asked Nat for another date. She agreed, and he took off.

When Herb was ready, I walked with him out back with to his father's Ford. He slipped in the driver's side, closed the door, and rolled down the window. Starting the motor, he gazed up at me and grinned. "You and I have had one *big* adventure, pal!"

He grinned. "Now, don't forget to be ready to make a talk at the picnic Friday."

Pulling away, he waved out the window. As the sedan turned toward town, I walked inside.

II

When I opened my eyes on Thursday morning, sunlight filled my room. Sitting up, I yawned, got out of bed, and hurried to the bathroom to clean myself up. Afterward, I got dressed in my school clothes. Sitting in my chair, I reflected on the Helen/Abigail predicament. Moments later a knock came to the door. It surprised me, because Nat usually doesn't get up as early as me.

"Come in," I said. The door opened, and Dad walked in. Closing the door, he sat on the side of my bed, facing me.

"Son, I don't want to impose. I see you're surprised, but I want to share something strange."

Dad did surprise me. When your father wants to talk to you alone, it's usually bad news, but I suppose you never know.

"What do you want, Dad? In a few minutes Aunt Cora will be calling us to breakfast."

His eyes twinkled. "Yes, but first, I had something odd happen last night. After our adventure with the German thugs, I wanted to share it with Helen, because … well, we have been talking about some plans, as you know, for the *future*."

I felt uneasy. "I don't know what to say."

Looking at the floor for a moment, he lifted his gaze to me. "Last night after dinner, I tried to call Helen from the living room. You know what?" He paused. "Her telephone rang twice, and then an operator said, 'I'm sorry, sir. That line is no longer in service.'

"Well … that *surprised me* but I thanked the operator and hung up."

Dad glanced out my window like he was searching for the right words. After a few seconds, he faced me again. "I decided to drive over to her place, which is a nice house she was renting in a good neighborhood. Going up on the porch, I saw a *For Rent* sign taped to the front door. About then I noticed a black sedan in the driveway, so I decided to knock. In no time a woman who looked to be in her 50s opened the door, and she gave me the once over.

"She wore the kind of faded blue dress a woman might wear when she's cleaning. A man with white hair and a long nose who was wearing overalls appeared, and he looked over her shoulder. She jerked her head at him and said, 'He's my husband. When we get the house ship-shape, he'll be glad to talk to you about terms.'

"To satisfy my curiosity, I told them I knew Helen LaSalle and her daughter Joyce. In fact, I said, 'We are more than friends, and I would like to know where she is.'

"The man shrugged his shoulders, and he said, 'You know as much as we do, young feller. She cleared outta here sometime last night, taking the little girl and their clothes and all their stuff with her.'

"In fact, he went on to say Helen owes them $75, so if I see her, I should tell her that she needs to pay the rent."

As Dad was explaining, I realized my visit likely caused Helen, or Abigail, or whatever her name is, to leave. I decided to play along. "Did she leave a forwarding address?"

Dad stared at me for a long minute. "Look, James. If you come across any information about Helen and Joyce, well, I'd like to have it. Right now, I'll confess she's making me angry."

From below we heard Aunt Cora's sing-song voice: "Hello, upstairs! Time for *breakfast*!"

"Let's go eat, son. But for now, you and I should keep this little matter *off the record*."

Nodding, I followed Dad downstairs. Sitting at the kitchen table with him and Nat and Aunt Cora, we ate breakfast pretty much as usual. I decided to think more before I spoke about Helen or Abigail, so I didn't say much.

Later, after Nat and I arrived at school, we just smiled at each other and left for our classes. I knew Thursday would be another easy day with our classes having discussions about the war and the Allies. And since I kept getting asked, I gave a sanitized summary of the violent thieves trying to rob us yesterday. Being the center of attention made my day a little awkward, but I mainly repeated my tale.

Herb and I are in more than one class together, and when asked, he gave a slightly different version. I said he was the "star" of our story, and I said he was the "hero," but the looks both of us received from so many girls made us feel like the most popular guys in school. I could tell Herb was basking in the glory! Come to think of it, I guess the glory pleased me too!

But without Jefferson baseball, life seemed to have a hole in it. On the way home that afternoon, I thought about our team, the experiences, and the friends. Parking the truck, I thought *I can't wait for summer baseball with the Broncos.*

I spent almost two hours hoeing the garden and cleaning the barn. Nat came out to the barn when I was nearly done, and she helped groom the horses, Lady and Midnight. I think Nat favors Lady, because she's a mare. I was too cautious to ride Midnight hard, but I understand Dad rode the big quarter horse in more than one county race back in the 1930s. These days both of the horses love the attention, and we just ride them once or twice a week.

Nat and I both finished our tasks at the same time, and she told me she and Ernie planned to see the Hitchcock movie *Shadow of a Doubt* on Friday evening.

She looked thoughtful. "I was afraid those crooks who were trying to rob us would scare Ernie away from our family, but afterward, he seemed okay, just a little nervous. He thought everyone handled it real well."

I've always had doubts about Ernie, but Nat seems quite interested in seeing *Shadow of a Doubt*. When I asked, she showed me a review she clipped from the *Charlottesville Record*.

I read it quickly. In the film, Teresa Wright plays Charlotte Newton, the star, and Joseph Cotton plays Charles Oakley, or "Uncle Charlie," the co-star. Seeing two men watching his house, Uncle Charlie secretly travels from New Jersey to California to visit his family, especially his niece, Charlotte, or "Charlie." She learns Uncle Charlie is one of two suspects in a murder, and he wants her to help find the *actual* murderer, denying that he's the killer. After reading the review, this Hitchcock movie sounds pretty good, and I want to see it too.

I looked up, and she smiled. "Ernie asked me to go yesterday, after the sheriff's deputies left with the prisoners. Today I found this review. So, I'll give Ernie another chance this Friday evening."

It occurred to me that maybe I should give him the benefit of the doubt. "Thinking about it, I'd like to see *Shadow of a Doubt* too. I'll ask Linda to go, but we'll go on Saturday. The baseball team is having our end-of-season get-together with the coaches tomorrow evening, and I can't miss that. But the Hitchcock movie sounds like a good mystery, and another good date for Saturday evening!"

Grinning, she took off upstairs, and I went into the kitchen to call Linda. Picking up the receiver, I had a bright idea. I'll ask if she can come to the baseball party on Friday *and* the movie on Saturday.

Feeling clever, I dialed her number, and Missus Lawton answered. I mentioned the baseball event, and she asked me to wait while she called Linda. Moments later, Linda asked, "How are you, James? Today at school all your buddies were talking about you and Herb and your folks having some crooks try to rob your family!"

Since I didn't see her at school today, I gave her the highlights. Before we finished, Linda agreed to my new idea of a "double date," in other words, two dates in two evenings. She asked her mother, and Missus Lawton gave the go-ahead. When we hung up, everything looked good.

I went up to my room, sat at my desk, and reflected on
Otto Herman. I sure hope he's gone forever from our
lives. On a more pressing point, I'm not going to say
anything to Dad about Helen, or Abigail. I decided the
less said, the better, and let the chips fall.

III

Friday was another swell day, because you have
to love the last day of school. By then everyone
has turned in books and cleaned out lockers, so
what's left is you go to each class, hear some well
wishes from teachers and friends, and pick up your
report card. I knew Dad would be happy with mine,
because I got all "A's," except in Geometry, where I
received a "B" from Miss Martin. But that doesn't
bother me, because I don't plan to be an engineer or a
scientist.

I think the most fun class is Mister Knudson and his
Geography class. Knudson, a six-foot, big-bodied,
outgoing teacher, is also an assistant football coach.
Coach Spencer is the head coach, Mister Shears
coaches the ends and running backs, and Mister
Jackson works with the linemen on offense and
defense. They say Coach Knudson is tough on the
players in practice, but you can't tell it by his casual,
upbeat demeanor in the classroom.

Anyway, today Mister Knudson seemed in a really
good mood, and he told some funny experiences that

happened last fall. With his blue eyes, black wavy hair, and quick wit, there are plenty of Jefferson guys and gals who like him. Anyway, I think the best story was about Jefferson's home game with Staunton last fall when Jack Jones, the quarterback, dropped back to pass, but both receivers and a halfback were covered. So Jack, who isn't afraid to take a risk, tucked the football under his arm and zigzagged through the defenders all the way to the goal line for a 76-yard touchdown, and along the way he picked up one block from every teammate!

Jack, as we all know, is a fun-loving junior who's also in my Geography and US History classes. When he trotted back to the Jefferson bench after his touchdown run, some of my friends said he yelled, "It's a good thing our receivers were covered, or I would have had to throw a good pass!"

After Mister Knudson's class ended, we all walked out feeling pretty good. I stopped and talked with a few friends in the hallway, and I met Nat around 3:15 n the parking lot. On the way home I concentrated on my driving, because the traffic was heavier than usual. But I listened to Nat going on and one like a broken record about Wanda and Linda and Iris and several more of her friends who are dating, most of them with ballplayers.

When I tried to change the subject, she gave me a long look like I knew nothing about dating. As we turned into our driveway, she surprised me. "James, I'm not certain I want to keep seeing Ernie. He's six years older than me, and he's not impressed with 'educated women.' Those are his words, not mine."

Climbing out of the pickup, we walked to the back porch. "Sis, you're not making a choice that will last forever." Even as I spoke, I had second thoughts because I don't like Ernie. So I added, "Just be sure he doesn't take you for a girl he can dominate because he's older."

When we walked into the kitchen, Aunt Cora smiled at us. "I hope you two have had a good day at school. It's the last day for 1943, right?"

"It sure was, Aunt Cora!" Nat offered her friendly smile, and she accepted when our aunt offered lemonade.

Taking the jug from the refrigerator, Aunt Cora looked at me. "James, you had a call from Linda, and a message, and I quote, 'Tell him I'll be ready by 5:00.' You understand that, right?"

"Yes, I do, Aunt Cora. I'll skip lemonade this time, because I have to go up and change for the baseball party." Stopping, I smiled. "Linda's coming with me. It's going to be at Coach Spencer's house. He and his wife Adell live in a big house near The Corner in town."

By the time I returned, my watch said 4:15. I sat down in the kitchen with Aunt Cora, and she poured me a glass of lemonade. Sitting down, she gave me a worried look. "That fellow Ernie picked up your sister a few minutes ago." She frowned. "I just *don't know* about him."

She hesitated. "You know, James, I got to thinking last year that I knew Otto Herman pretty well, and at one point, maybe too well. He tried to go *too far* one time, so I quit seeing him."

She had my attention, and I listened carefully. "Afterward, I was sorry I ever met Otto. The few times I've seen this fellow Ernie, I see qualities, and I can't explain it, but they make me feel he's *like* Otto." She shook her head. "He could be related, except I never heard Otto talk about being married, or that he had kids. Have you?"

When I shook my head no, Aunt Cora dropped the subject. She just smiled sweetly, and I smiled back. Still, I thought *She sees intuitively something about Ernie she can't put into words. I can't identify it either, but I think she's right.*

Glancing at my watch, I jumped up. "Thanks for the lemonade, Aunt Cora, and thanks for the insight, too." I went around the table, leaned over, and kissed her on the cheek. She looked up, and I saw in her eyes what I can only describe as a mother's love.

At the kitchen door, I turned and smiled. "See you later, and I hope you have a nice evening!"

She gazed at me with her eyes sparkling, and I headed for the Chevy. Starting the engine, I pulled out the driveway and drove toward Linda's house thinking *This is turning into a really good evening.*

Twenty minutes later, I knocked on the Lawton's door. Linda answered, and she was wearing a blue skirt and a pale blue blouse with a fluffy collar. She had her hair brushed neatly into the Victory Roll, some blue shadow on her eyes, a touch of lipstick on her lips, and the hint of blush on her cheeks. Looking at her took away my breath.

"Come on, James! Don't just stand there *gawking*!"

Grabbing my hand, she led me to the Chevy, her face wreathed in a smile. I held her door, hurried around, and got into the driver's place. Starting the engine, we headed for the coach's house, located just off University Avenue. On the way Linda asked me about the baseball team and my friends who play ball.

She touched my right arm. "I think Walt is taking Wanda to this picnic. She told me he called her after school, and she accepted. She sounded pretty excited!"

Turning onto University Avenue at The Corner, I grinned. "Oddly enough, Wanda is one of Nat's best friends, and Walt is one of my best friends."

Looking across the street, Linda said: "Don't look now, James, but there's your sister, over there by the Chancellor's Building, talking to some guy. Is he the new boyfriend? I heard she was seeing some guy from England."

As I slowed down, she took another look. "I think they're *arguing*, but I can't hear what they're saying. I hope Nat's okay. "

I decided to park across the street and check. With our windows rolled down, we could hear Nat and Ernie's voices. But neither of us could understand more than a word or two. I saw his black Buick parked at the curb beside them. My mind flashed back to my visit to Ernie's upstairs apartment in the Chancellor's Building, and I wondered if they were going there.

As we watched, they seemed to speak louder like they were arguing. Ernie reached out his hand to her, but we saw her knock it away. He said something, and in a flash, Nat slapped his face, and we heard the *smack*. She turned and walked away.

For a second or two, Ernie seemed stunned, but he took off after her. Taking long strides, he caught up with her, grabbed her arm, and jerked her, spinning her around to face him. In her momentum, she fell against him, and they both stumbled, and in a moment they recovered. Nat began pounding Ernie's chest with her fists, and he stood there taking it. But after a few seconds, he wrapped his arms tightly around her, and she quieted down.

I didn't understand what I was seeing, and Linda turned to me. "I don't get it."

We watched as Ernie took Nat's hand, led her back to the car, helped her into the passenger's seat, and, looking around, he hurried around climbed in the driver's seat. We heard the engine roar, and the car sped off in the direction of downtown.

Starting my engine, I said, "Linda, we're gotta follow them! I'm concerned about Nat!"

"*Do it*, James! I think that guy hurt her, and now he's dragging her off somewhere!"

Accelerating, I drove after the black Buick. When he turned onto Main Street, I closed the gap to half a block. He turned the Buick into the parking lot of the Blue Ridge Hotel, and parked. Both of them climbed out of the car. I slowed the Chevy as we approached the hotel, and Linda and I watched. Nat seemed to be going willingly with Ernie as they walked around to the front and entered the front door of the three-story hotel.

Stopping, I looked over the old brick building with its heavy glassed door, long maroon awning covering the sidewalk, concrete lintels topping the narrow windows, and sculpted cornices lining the flat roof. At one time the hotel may have been first class, but not these days.

Linda observed: "It looks like Nat went along with him. I didn't see her resisting. I don't get it." She looked at me. "Do you still think she's in danger?"

"I'm gonna follow them and find out, just to make sure." I glanced at her. "Linda, you can help me figure out what's happening."

Turning around, I parked in the hotel lot. Locking the Chevy, we walked around to the front and went inside. I could see the lobby had a high white ceiling, light maroon walls, several large portraits of historical Virginia leaders, including three of Thomas Jefferson, and a long mahogany front desk. Behind the desk a middle aged balding man in a blue suit and maroon necktie peered at us through horn-rimmed glasses.

Linda whispered, "Why don't you ask at the desk if Ernie is registered here?"

"Good idea," I murmured. As I walked to the front desk, the clerk studied me like I might be an enemy agent. At his elbow I noticed a brass nameplate saying *V.T. Cavalier*

"May I help you, sir?" His voice was nasal, and he displayed a holier-than-thou attitude.

I ignored the attitude. "Yes, sir. I'm looking for Mister Ernie Herbert. He came in here not long ago with my sister. She's a nice-looking brunette who's too young to stay in a hotel."

After peering at me, he opened a large ledger with pale green covers. Turning a few pages, he stopped and scanned a page. "We have no 'Ernie Herbert' registered, sir."

"Look, Mister. I just watched the guy walk through the front entrance not five minutes ago. As I said, he has my underage sister with him. You *must* have seen them!"

Unfazed, Mister Cavalier looked down his nose at me. "You may be referring to a Mister *Erich Arnold.* Mister Arnold is the only registered guest to enter the lobby in the past thirty minutes."

Looking around, I noticed a bellhop waiting at the end of the counter. Looking again, I recognized him as Danny Lincoln, the guy Herb, Walt, and I once helped fight three bullies outside Sammy's.

"Mister Baker," Danny said, "The man you're looking for just got on the elevator. He's registered in room 202."

"Thanks, Danny," I replied, grabbing Linda's hand. "Let's go upstairs and find Nat."

We hurried to the elevator, pressed the button for 2, and waited several seconds. The doors slid open, and a dark-haired woman with wire-rimmed glasses and a wry smile pulled open the metal gate. "Floor, *please*?"

"Two," I replied, smiling at her curious gaze. She closed the doors and the gate, pulled the lever, and the lift moved slowly upward, bumping to a stop at 2. Opening the door and the gate, she smiled at us like we were familiar guests.

Once in the hall, the doors closed, and I spotted a wall sign with an arrow pointing toward rooms 201-210. Linda and I walked over to 202, and both of us listened at the door. After a few seconds we could hear quiet sobs like someone was crying. I knocked three times, and waited. After what seemed a long wait, the door opened slightly, and Nat's eyes peeked out at us. The door flew open, and she came and hugged me, crying, "James, oh, James … I'm so glad you're here!"

Looking over my shoulder, Nat said, "Hi, Linda." She smiled quickly. "Come in you two."

We walked in, and I closed the door. We saw Ernie, or whatever his name is, sitting on the side of the bed. His sandy hair was disheveled like he'd been in a fight. His pale cheeks were red, his blue eyes teary, and his Nordic features looked distraught.

Nat went over and took his right hand in hers. He stared at us, his eyes moving between me and Linda and Nat, and back to me. "I've made a terrible mistake." He took a deep breath. "*Mein Gott*, I've made the worst mistake of my life."

He began to cry, and we watched the tears pour down his high cheeks. The crying continued for a couple of minutes, before he pulled a handkerchief from a back pocket, dried the tears, and tried to smile.

"Tell them what you told me," Nat said, and sadness permeated her soft voice.

He nodded. "Yes, my true name is Erich Arnold. My mother is Ann Arnold, an English woman who was never married to my father, a German you knew as Otto Herman. He abandoned us two weeks after I was born, and later my mother told me about it. She raised me for a few years in Munich, but when the Depression came, she moved us to Portsmouth, England, because she had a brother there. I finished public school in England in 1939, and the world war began a few months later. Living and working in Portsmouth, I used to ask about my father. One day my mother learned from a friend that he emigrated to America, and she told me what she knew."

Erich took a deep breath. "I made up my mind to travel to America and find Otto Herman. When I let my mother know, she wanted to help, but she had very little information. She did remember Otto had a married sister living in New York City. She also found an address that she once wrote in her diary, 'just in case.' So that was my starting point: A name, Elsa Ellis, who was married to Lionel Ellis, and an address twenty years old. Earlier this year, I landed a job on a merchant ship. On the way across the Atlantic, I decided when I arrived, I would tell people I was an English student looking for an American college. Since America is allied with England and at war with Germany, I figured the less I said about my German background, the better.

"When I landed in New York City, I became Ernie Herbert. A day later I found the address my mother gave me, and I knocked on the apartment door. I had no idea what to expect. When the door was opened, a teenager who was younger than me asked what I wanted. In a flash I devised the tale that a fellow living at New York University named him as a student who could advise me on local colleges. He accepted that, introduced himself as Karl Ellis, and invited me in. We sat down and talked about colleges in New York. He opened up so easily, I think, because he's lonely. We kept exchanging things about our background for an hour. By then we both had consumed a bottle of beer, and I think we liked each other.

"I learned as much as I could, starting with the fact that Karl's mother Elsa died of pneumonia a few years ago. He was living in the apartment with his father, who is a chemist working on some project for the US government. Karl told me he's a sophomore at NYU, which was located nearby, and he liked college life.

"He offered me another beer, and he got one for himself too. He was feeling good, and he started telling me about his trip to Virginia and his 'adventure,' as he called it, which resulted in the death of Otto Herman. Hearing my father was dead, I was shocked, but I hid my reaction. Karl went on to say his uncle 'betrayed' his adopted country, so I figured secrets were involved. He shifted to talking about his good friends in Charlottesville, Natalia and James Baker.

"The way you two fitted you into his adventure suggested that you were connected to Otto's death. At that point I sensed Karl was getting nervous, because he went back to talking about his college activities. But I had heard enough, and I decided to come to Charlottesville and find what actually happened to my father."

Erich looked at us for a long moment. "When I arrived in Charlottesville, I found an apartment, unpacked my bags, located the city library, and did some research in old newspapers. A couple of newspaper stories said Otto Herman and Derek Miller were shot near Charlottesville in 1942, but the papers didn't provide many details. Still, Karl had revealed more than he realized, and putting it all together, I set out to kill you two and avenge my father's death.

"But the more I learned about Otto's personal history, the more I understood he and Derek were vicious Nazis. They almost certainly would have killed Natalia and Karl, but instead, James, you shot Otto, and Natalia, you shot him too, when he tried to kill your brother."

At that point Erich seemed to run out of gas. He stood up, excused himself, and went into the adjoining bathroom, closing the door. We listened to the sound of running water, and then we heard nothing for a couple of minutes. I think we all wondered about Erich. At that point, the door opened and he emerged, his face scrubbed, his hair combed, and his countenance bright.

"Why don't you call me Erich? You know the name 'Ernie Herbert' is an alias I invented to come here and look for you." Moving his eyes between Nat and me, he offered a weak smile.

Nat spoke first. "Erich, I'm going with my brother and his girlfriend Linda, and we're headed to a party. I've heard your story, but I can't claim to understand it, not really. I need time to think."

Erich shrugged his shoulders. "Well, maybe it's too late, Natalia, for us to be friends. I plan on returning to New York City and telling Karl Ellis who I really am. After all, we're first cousins. Actually, I need to return to England and contribute to the war effort against the Nazis."

Smiling quickly, Nat turned to me. "James, let's get going to the baseball picnic. I'll have friends there, and I'd like to help celebrate your undefeated season!"

Linda hugged Nat, and I thought both of them might cry, but Linda grinned. "C'mon, Nat. I know James is late." She pointed to a clock on the end table. "It's about ten minutes to 6:00, and they started an hour ago."

I nodded at Ernie, opened the door, and the three of us left. The last I saw of Erich Arnold, he was sitting on the bed watching us leave his room. It looked like he was crying again. Like Nat, I've thought about what to do about Erich, but evidently we're no longer targets.

Reaching the elevator, I pressed the button, and the doors opened. As we stepped inside, I looked at the girls. "You two are going to like my friends and teammates!"

The doors closed, the dark-haired operator grinned, and we descended slowly. After a bump, the doors opened, she pulled the gate open, and we stepped into the lobby. With one girl holding each of my hands, we walked past the desk clerk and outside into the beautiful evening

Chapter 13

Yesterday and Tomorrow

Coach Spencer and his wife Adell live in a large white two-story Victorian located two streets off Main Street, a few blocks from the high school. Linda, Nat, and I arrived shortly after 6:00, and parked cars lined both sides of the street. Luckily I found a parking space a few houses away. The three of us hopped out of the Chevrolet and walked quickly to the Spencer's home. Around the side, we came to a gate in the picket fence that surrounded the backyard.

At the gate we met Adell, the coach's wife. A short, friendly brunette with an upbeat personality, she stood beside two other smiling women. "Well," Adell declared, "hello, there! You're late, but come in and join the fun! The coaches are in back by our two picnic tables. Your friends have a head start eating, so you're just in the nick of time!"

Turning to her companions, Adell introduced Mabel Jackson, a slender brunette with black eyes and a round face wreathed in smiles. "Hi, there," she said. "You don't know me, but I'm Clyde's better half. The hamburgers and hot dogs are going fast!"

After we greeted Missus Jackson, Adell introduced the third woman. "This is Clara, Ray Riley's wife!"

They grinned at each other, and Clara smiled at us. "We're all good friends. Between us, we've seen more high school ball games than any three women in Virginia!"

We greeted Missus Riley. A petite blonde with a cute face, blue eyes, and a red ribbon around her hair, she nodded. "Hello from me, too!"

Waving toward the yard behind the house, her eyes seemed to dance. "Ray's at the barbecue, and he's grilled three dozen hamburgers already! Everyone thinks he just drives a bus and helps the coaches, but nobody goes hungry around my Ray!"

While Adell, Mabel, and Clara laughed gloriously, Coach Spencer saw us and waved. "Come on in, and find a place! The ladies are gonna give you a paper plate and a hamburger or a hot dog, so you'd better get started. Herb and Jack think this is an eating contest, and they're batting 1.000! Walt and Bob and Scott don't want to be left out, and they're gaining on the big guys!"

Moving over to the first long pine table, I sat on the same bench as Herb and Jack and Walt and Damon. On the other side sat more big eaters: Bob, Andy, Dave, and John Kilpatrick, the sophomore. Matt Richards and Rob Henry stood at the far end of the table, holding their plates, munching hot dogs, and sipping Coca-Cola in paper cups.

The second long table held the girls. Taking a look, I saw Iris Hofner, Wanda Winston, Claudia Rogers, and Annette Wimmer. I've haven't met Annette, but she's a good-looking blonde sophomore who plays softball, stars in basketball, and dates John Kilpatrick. I noticed a few other girls from school, but I didn't know their names. All of them had plates of food, cups of Coca-Cola, and they were chatting and laughing about baseball, dates, movies, and whatever came to mind. Nat and Linda, both smiling, made a beeline for that table. I think the mood got even more light-hearted.

"Well, look here," declared Coach Jackson. "James has finally arrived, and with good news. He brought two girls to join the fun!"

Everyone laughed at the dumb joke, and Walt stood up and waved. "Okay, everyone! I know what happened. The old Baker pickup finally broke down, but no matter. We're all done *practicing* for 1943!"

Another round of laughter followed, and Missus Spencer brought me a paper plate with a hamburger, a scoop of coleslaw, and some potato chips. Missus Jackson brought a pan of baked beans and spooned me a scoop, and Missus Riley brought a cup of lemonade. Across from me Herb, grinning widely, stood up. Raising his cup of Coke, he yelled, "Let's all drink to James, the best high school relief pitcher in Virginia!"

More yells and clapping followed, and the party proceeded happily. Coach Spencer walked around making lighthearted comments to each of the guys, and Coach Jackson kept coming around to ask who needed a hamburger or a hot dog. Wearing a white's chef's hat, Ray Riley stood at the grill with a long-handed spatula, turning hamburgers, rolling hot dogs, and smiling.

A little while after the last person finished eating, Coach Spencer raised his hand. "All right, everyone. We're going to have our annual awards ceremony."

He stood at the end of the first table, waiting for everyone to have a seat. Several folding chairs were placed at the far end of the tables, and Ray Riley and the three wives sat those.

"Coach Jackson and I have talked about who wins what award," Coach Spencer stated. "Of course, the school paid for everything. There's a jeweler downtown who engraves these trophies. Three cheers for our principal, Mister Marcus Redberry, who took care of the payment!"

Suddenly the back yard was filled with clapping and yelling, "*Three cheers for Mister Redberry*! Hip, hip, hooray!!"

Herb stood up and yelled, "Let's' do it again, *louder*!"

"*Three cheers for Mister Redberry*!"

Nearby a dog barked, and Coach Spencer grinned. He held up an award with a foot-high brass statue of a baseball player swinging a bat. The award was mounted on a polished oak base with an engraved nameplate. "This one's for the Most Valuable Player, and it goes to … *Herb Jenkowski*! C'mon up here, *Herb*!"

Herb looked surprised, and his face reddened, but he stood up, looked around, and nodded. He made his way to Coach Spencer, who handed him the trophy with his name engraved on the nameplate. Taking it, Herb thanked both coaches and shook their hands vigorously.

Turning to face us, he smiled. "I've never had more fun playing on a high school team than this baseball team. I'm proud of our season!"

Lowering his head to hide tears, he returned to the table, sat on the bench, and, when someone asked, he passed the trophy along for everyone to see. I saw Iris at the other table with her eyes on Herb, and she had the biggest smile. In a moment Herb spotted her, and winked.

"Next, we have the Hitter of the Year. And you know, we may be splitting hairs here, but we decided to award this one to … *Jack Jones*!"

I looked at Jack, and he was shaking his head and blushing. Smiling, Coach Spencer continued: "Come up here, *Jack!*"

Getting slowly to his feet, Jack strolled up to the coach. I thought he looked a little embarrassed, and if so, that's a first. Nothing ever bothers Jack. When Coach Spencer handed him the trophy, he just gazed at it for a few moments. Holding it up, he grinned. "I'm really *glad* I could contribute to this team … this is a *really* good team …" and he broke down.

Gripping the trophy in his right hand, Jack pulled out a handkerchief to wipe away the tears. Everyone around me felt moved by the sight, because Jack, and, of course, Herb, they're two tough hombres. From the other table, Claudia was smiling at him. When he regained his composure, Jack nodded and flicked a smile at her, indicating he would see her later.

"We had a good idea for a new award," Coach Spencer said, after Jack sat down. "This one we're calling the Most Improved Player, and we believe it must go to *Bob James*! C'mon, Bob! You had a swell season too!"

I looked over and Bob had the classic expression of *Who, me?* Guys on both sides of him pushed him to get up and go accept the trophy, and after a minute, he stood and made it to Coach Spencer.

The coach looked around at us. "This one was a hard choice too, because several of you have *really improved*." He grinned. "I don't see how we could have had a *better* bunch of young men … right, Clyde?"

Smiling, Coach Jackson looked around. "I'm proud as I can be to help Coach Spencer. I don't think I've ever met a finer man, or a better coach. Three cheers for Coach Spencer! And three cheers for our great baseball team!"

The yard was filled with yelling and cheering, and again the women and girls joined the racket! I glanced over at Coach Spencer, and he looked humbled. Tears trickled down his cheeks as he bowed his head. Finally, he spoke, in barely audible tones. "Thank you all, each and every one of you."

Taking a deep breath, the coach declared, "Well, now, last but not least, we're gonna give this award for Best Pitcher to … *James Baker*!"

I looked at the coach, and he was all smiles. Suddenly a wave of emotion struck me like a bolt of lightning. In a moment Herb was on one side and Jack on the other, and they hauled me up by the arms. All three of us paraded up to the coach, and once we got there, Herb and Jack grinned, released me, and returned to their seats.

I think Coach Spencer knew what Herb and Jack had in mind, and he just grinned. All at once I knew why the others who received a trophy felt so emotional. My teammates were laughing, joking, and congratulating me.

Suddenly Herb stood up and said, "C'mon, James! Let's have a *speech*!"

Several others jumped to their feet, Herb counted to 3, and they said in unison. "Go, James! *Speak for Jefferson!*"

Looking around, I tried to smile. "Well, I have to say all of us have been fortunate this year. Everyone here, and I do mean *every single one*, contributed to our exceptional team. But I know the rest of you join me in saying that without two really first-rate coaches, Coach Spencer and Coach Jackson, and all the help the whole team gets from Mister Riley ..."

Pausing, I mustered my strength. "Our season shows everyone how *real good teamwork* and *real good coaching* can help each and every one of us be better players and better teammates, and if you guys feel like me, you know we'll never forget our season ..."

At that point I couldn't say any more. Tears filled my eyes, I bowed my head, and I headed back to my place. When I sat down, Herb said, "James, you gotta pass your trophy around, too!"

He grabbed the brass award, stood up, and held it over his head. "Three cheers for James, a guy who can hit a baseball so far it might end up in your *pocket*!"

The whole backyard filled with cheering, clapping, and laughing, and Herb handed the award to Jack. He took a quick look, and stood up. "You don't want to bat against James, with tricky ol' Herb behind the plate calling the pitches. No sir! If they get you in a pinch, especially with two strikes, just look out! James winds up, and here comes that nasty *drop ball*, and you swing, and think you'll club that pitch, but no! Your bat's got a *hole* in it, and you're swinging at air! And back of the plate, Herb's got the ball in that big mitt, and he's smiling behind that mask. And you feel like hiding somewhere. And you walk away, and you look out there, and there stands James, with that innocent smile, and brother! It's just *better luck next time*!!"

A bigger wave of cheering, clapping, and laughter rolled over me, and I felt my cheeks burning. I waved my hand, but no words came. I felt overwhelmed, as the guys around me kept congratulating me. I glanced at the girls' table, and I saw Nat with tears rolling down her cheeks. When she saw me looking at her, she mouthed the words *You're the best brother ever.*

An hour or so later I caught up with Linda, who kept smiling, and we spotted Nat, who was chatting happily with Bob James. Saying our goodbyes, Bob took off, and I walked with Linda and Nat to the Chevy parked down the street. We got in, I started the engine, and we headed for Linda's house. Once there, she and I climbed out, and I walked her up to the front porch. I started to speak, but she grabbed my face with both hands, and we kissed long and hard. Afterward, Linda gave me another dreamy smile, and moments later she disappeared inside.

I walked slowly back to the car feeling elated, and I realized what friends like Herb and Jack meant when they said, "I'm on Cloud Seven!" Nat was waiting in the car, and she grinned when I climbed in. Sighing, I started the car, pulled into the street, and headed for home. Neither of us said much on the way.

Instead, I reflected on the remarkable events of the party, and I hoped everyone else had plenty of fun too. I smiled about the kidding I received from the guys. The memorable ceremony for the 1943 baseball team and receiving the Best Pitcher Award is one of the fun reasons that high school sports mean so much to so many people at schools all over the country.

II

On Friday evening at 8:30, I turned into our driveway, parked the Chevrolet across from the front porch, and Dad and Aunt Cora were sitting in two of the wooden chairs with the porch light glowing above them. Seeing them, Nat grabbed my award. We climbed out of the car, walked toward the porch, and she remarked, "Bob James wants me to go to the movies with him on Saturday."

She sounded pleased, and I stopped. "That sounds good. Are you going?"

Nat stopped too. "*Of course*! Bob is *really nice*, and he's *very handsome*. Now I'll have another reason to go to your baseball games!"

Looking ahead, I saw Dad and Aunt Cora watching us. Each of them was holding a tall glass, likely filled with lemonade. He made a comment to her, and we saw them laughing.

I murmured: "It looks like Dad and Aunt Cora are having a good time."

"Yes, so I see" Nat replied, keeping her voice low. "We'll soon see *how good*, right?"

Reaching the porch, we climbed the steps, and I saw Dad peering at Nat and the trophy. Smiling, he tinkled the ice in his glass. "So tell us about baseball party."

Before I could reply, Aunt Cora set her glass down beside her. "James, you look like the cat that caught the canary!" She offered her innocent smile. "Did something *good* happen?"

"Actually, yes, real good ..."

Nat interrupted, placing the trophy in my hands. "Go on, Big Brother. Tell them!"

The bright porch light likely revealed my tears, but I plunged ahead. "At our baseball picnic I received this trophy for Best Pitcher, and ..."

Nat couldn't wait. "I went to the picnic at Coach Spencer's house too, and I can tell you, James was *really surprised*!"

Dad grinned. "What a swell way to end your baseball season! Of course, I know Coach Spencer and Coach Jackson, and they're first-rate fellows. Those two are a *big part* of Jefferson sports."

A look of contentment graced Aunt Cora's face. After Dad's comment, she looked at us. "Well, we have some news, too, and I must say today has been exceptional." She hesitated, and her eyes filled with tears. Suddenly she grabbed Dad's hand.

"You tell them, Zeke. I'm not sure I can …"

Squeezing her hand and smiling, Dad looked at us. "I'm glad you two have returned, and …"

Leaning forward, Aunt Cora interrupted: "Your father has asked me to *marry him*!"

Giving us a radiant smile, she seemed bursting with pride. "It's been quite a while since my Joseph passed away, and I was invited to come and live with you all, and a lot of water has passed under the bridge. But, today I'm the *happiest woman* in Charlottesville!"

We could see both of them were feeling emotional, especially Aunt Cora, whose eyes looked teary. Dad cleared his throat. "First, let me say what you already know, that I spent some time getting acquainted with and seeing Helen LaSalle."

Pulling a handkerchief from his back pocket, he dabbed at his eyes. "I felt like I needed to do that, because it's been a long time since I thought much about another woman. Actually, I seldom fund a reason to do that since your mother was killed by the drunk driver six years ago."

As he spoke, I stood there and thought *Our lives are about to take a major shift, and Nat and I will have an aunt and a stepmother, all in one great woman.*

After a pause, Dad looked at us. "After we stopped those three thugs who came here to rob us, I tried to call Helen and let her know what happened. I dialed her number, but the operator came on and said the telephone had been disconnected. Of course, I wondered why, so I hopped in the car and drove over to Helen's house. I found that the husband and wife who rent the house were cleaning it. When I asked, they told me Missus LaSalle and her daughter disappeared the night before. In fact, she left *owing money.*"

He frowned. "As a matter of fact, I already had made my decision. I just wanted to let Helen know that I decided to pursue my relationship with my sister-in-law Cora Raleigh, instead of with her, meaning Helen. There you have it in a nutshell."

Dad looked at Aunt Cora, and she kept her hand in his. "I guess you can tell she agreed!"

The two of them stood up. "First," Aunt Cora said, "I can't be unfair to either of you. You're my only sister's children, and I've always felt like more than an aunt to you."

She cleared her throat. "So I have to ask a question that bothers me."

Nat grinned. "Okay, go ahead."

Aunt Cora studied her. "Who is this *Ernie* person you brought to the house?" She raised her eyebrows. "When I look at him, I see a younger Otto Herman. *Why* is that?"

Sighing, Nat nodded. "Well, Ernie Herbert's real name is Erich Arnold, and you're right. I found out he is the *son* of Otto Herman. Last Saturday he drove me up to the old mountain cabin and, well, he pushed me into reconstructing just what his father made me do."

I interrupted. "You might as well know that Ernie, or Erich, came to America originally to find his father, who he had never seen. When he learned his real father was dead, he made up his mind to kill Nat and me, on the grounds that we killed him."

Nat rolled her eyes. "I was going to ease into that. Yes, Otto's son did plan to kill us, which I later learned led to the trip to the cabin, but our friend Cecil showed up and stopped him."

She paused briefly. "Earlier this evening, Erich took me to the hotel where he's now staying, but as it happened, James and Linda were going to the baseball get-together, and they spotted me talking to him near The Corner. They followed us, and if needed, my Big Brother would have saved my life *again*. But, it turned out there wasn't any need for that."

She sighed. "I guess I can take credit for Erich's change of heart. He said after I became upset at the cabin from all those awful memories, he realized for the first time how badly his father treated me, and how much I suffered. He admitted that he came close to harming me, but about that time, Cecil walked in the door with the .38 revolver sticking out of his pants pocket."

She shook her head. "Ernie, or Erich, told me at that moment he gave up the plan of avenging his father. He told me his decision was reinforced when those armed men came to our house, and he realized they were followers of Otto. To atone for what his father did, Erich says he will return to England and contribute to the war effort against Hitler and the Nazis. Anyway, James and Linda and I left Erich at the hotel, but now we know his true identity."

Nat sighed. "Yes, I wised up, *finally*. After that, I went with James and Linda to the baseball party. I'm *done* with Otto's son. Hopefully, we're done forever with Otto and Erich and that family!"

Dad started to reply, but Aunt Cora touched his arm. "In case you're wondering, my intuition told me that that Ernie guy was up to *no good*, and I was *right*!"

She smiled. "So, you two," and she hesitated. "You two need to tell us how you feel about this decision for us to *marry*. It means a great deal to me, you know, to have your support."

I smiled at her and Dad. "I've thought for some time you were both coming to the same conclusion. As for me, *I like it*."

I stepped over and hugged Aunt Cora. Tears flowed down her cheeks, but she smiled too. "Thank you, James. You don't know how much you two *mean* to me …"

Unable to say more, she wept, and Nat embraced her. "Please don't cry, Aunt Cora. I can't imagine Dad finding a better wife for himself or a better stepmother for us."

My sister broke into tears, too. She and Aunt Cora hugged each other tighter, and I felt awkward watching them. After a few moments, I turned to Dad. "I hope that answers your questions. Nat and I have talked about you and Aunt Cora more than once. We say "*Go for it!*"

By then the starry sky overhead seemed to be casting magic on our lives. My sister and I felt closer than ever to Dad, Aunt Cora, and to each other. We had gone from being teen targets to teen stars, the center of Zeke and Cora's universe. So in this wartime year, our last day of school was not only one fine day, but also one most memorable day.

9 7 9 8 9 9 9 3 1 0 9 0 2 2